It's a Long Ride to Texas, Baby

It's a Long Ride to Texas, Baby

A Novella

Katy Soljak

Press

Published by 99% Press,
an imprint of Lasavia Publishing Ltd.
Auckland, New Zealand
www.lasaviapublishing.com

Paintings by Katy Soljak
Songs: *Denton* and *Heaven* by Katy Soljak
Photos of paintings by Dru Burger
Cover design and layout by Daniela Gast

Also by the author 'My First Real Pash and Other Stories'.

ISBN: 978-1-99-116050-8

For SG

ACKNOWLEDGEMENTS

My publishers at Lasavia Publishing are first to be thanked. They believed in me and launched my first book of short stories in 2021. Now thanks to their further belief in me for releasing this novella. Rowan Johnson (aka Rowan Sylva) and Daniela Gast have been enthusiastic, fun to work with and professional. Being writers themselves, they picked up on some plot details and helped tweak them. They are a great team and I was thrilled to work with them again. Big thanks to my dedicated proof-readers, George Gardner and Susi Newborn, both British, who wrangled with my Spanglish dialogue at times but came through like champs and wrote excellent testimonials. Thanks to Thomas D Adelman for his outstanding testimonial and for contributing to the novella's story line.

Thanks to my first born, Sarah Gillett, whose love, beauty and wicked humour enhance my life's journey. A special thanks to my grandson, Sekoya Gillett, for his astute eye, humour and love. Also for being my first art critic. Thanks to his father Miles Gillett for his constant aroha, support and superb posters. Big posthumous thanks to my first husband, Bob Gillett for turning me on to Kenneth Patchen and Kurt Vonnegut and encouraging me to find an authentic voice in my writing. Muchas gracias to my second husband Carlos G Matos for his assistance with Spanish language, bringing me into the Latin community and always being available online during the writing of this novella. Thanks to all my sisters, Shona Whyte, Moira Lewis and Wendy

Dobson, who constantly check in on me offering their sisterly support and aroha. Thanks to darling Kararaina Penehira (wifey), who is constant aroha on my journey. Thanks to my niece Fiona Whyte for her love and support and for being the first family member to buy a painting.

Thanks to my dear friend Greer Dyson for making me part of her family and for writing a heartfelt testimonial. Thanks to Melissa Askham for her constant aroha and for keeping my hair looking fab. Thanks to Robyn Barrie for being an incredible yoga teacher all through the pandemic, keeping my body and mind in tune (at least on Mondays and Wednesdays). Thanks to my dear friend Kelley Diener for her art mentoring, having my back through some challenging times and for an excellent testimonial. Thanks to Anne Bailey, whose kindness, stillness and empathy have helped me on this journey. Thanks to Julie Biuso for her friendship and first class teamwork with the Song and Poetry Thing. Thanks to Susie Hunter for maintaining a warm and affordable home and putting up with my many creative projects over the years. Thanks to all my family, both blood and extended, who all enrich my life just by being in it. Finally thanks to my beautiful island Waiheke, for it's inspiration and supportive community. My Turangawaewae.

'and there's nothing so lonesome,
nothing quite so sad
than pulling into Denton at midnight
with your whole life in a bag.'

Tex-Mex Border July 1975

Johnny grabs Gala's arm and pulls her out of the garage. He is panic-white in the face and his eyes are wide.

'Quick get your kid. *Andeles, mija*, these guys are bad news!'

'Is he all right, Johnny? Shouldn't we...?'

Johnny's not listening. He's revving up the Mustang as Gala gets in with Leah and peels out from Jesús's driveway, wheels burning rubber. Lights flicker on in the house next door. Faces come to the window. The Mustang heads down Main Street and they're back on the freeway in seconds.

Johnny slows to an idling stop at the border gate after gunning at 120mph. The engine purrs like a jaguar as the border cop comes over to the window. He's armed and serious in an army-green uniform, bullet-proof vest, fully loaded with a colt 45, walkie-talkie and assorted survivor tools.

'*Hola, Señor*, what's the purpose of your trip to Mexico? Oh, hi Johnny. *Como estás, hombre?*'

The agent's face brightens, and the two men catch up in Spanish like old friends. Gala sees the agent look over at her. He nudges Johnny and laughs. She's feeling embarrassed and a little scared, not understanding what they are saying. She guesses that they are talking about Johnny's family. Then the agent stamps Johnny's passport, slaps the hood of the Mustang, gives Johnny a thumbs up and they drive through on to Mexican soil.

The temperature's rising and Johnny cranks up the air-conditioning. They're not talking about the fight. Gala feels sick and deathly afraid. She cradles Leah, smelling her little-girl-shampoo smell, trying to blot out the memory of the whole scene. Johnny is still pale, sweating and talking fast - still coked-up.

Denton Texas June 1975

The Greyhound hisses into the deserted bus station around midnight. Gala struggles down the steps, balancing her sleeping child on one hip, guitar over one shoulder and a worn suitcase in her hand.

'Y'all take care now Miss and watch that kid.'

'It looks closed.' Gala looks around the empty station. She's tired and scared.

'Yep, sure is, someone'll be here in the morning. Small town Denton, good luck!'

The cowboy bus driver smiles a tired smile as he cranks the long silver bus into gear. He's waiting for the only other passenger, a young black student in sweatshirt and jeans, to disembark.

The student lights up a cigarette standing under the single light, buzzing with moths. The crickets are deafening. Gala sits on the bench, her guitar propped up against the wall and holds her daughter Leah. She bites her bottom lip and watches as the long beam from a police car floodlight swings over her and on to the student.

'Everything all right, Ma'am?' an older Texan cop leans, leering out of the police car window.

'Actually, I need a taxi to a motel. Could you help me please, Sir?

The cop nods and grabs his walkie-talkie, watching the

student as he orders a cab.

'What about you boy? Y'all right?'

The young man puts his head down and walks quickly down the battered sidewalk into the swampy shadows of the unlit street.

'OK, Cab will be here for you in five minutes. Y'all take care, Miss.'

The police car slides off slowly in the direction of the young man.

Gala breathes out a sigh as the long green taxicab finally pulls up to the curb.

'Do you know a motel around here? Not too expensive?' she asks the driver.

'Sure, the Paradise Motel is a good price for what you get.'

'OK, thanks, that'll do.'

The driver gets out and helps with her suitcase, throwing it in the trunk. Gala climbs in the back seat and settles, Leah and the guitar next to her. She relaxes for a moment in the spongy vinyl back seat. A young fresh-faced Texan, smelling of too much Brut, a Marine haircut and Burger Boy cap, leans over from the front. His bright smile lights up like a lamp in the dark cab, eyes bugging out, shining, pure cheese ball innocence.

'You must be a rock star from England or somethin' with your guitar an' all and that funny way you talk. Will you sign my cap?'

Gala is flattered and laughs up at the boy. 'New Zealand actually, I'm not famous but I'll sign your cap if you like.'

The cab slows down outside the Paradise Motel. It's bungalow style, in faded turquoise with a flashing pink neon sign. A small red light bulb beckons above the office. Gala notices the vacancy sign is hanging slightly askew as she drags her suitcase and sleepy child into the office. She rings the 'old school' bell on the counter and waits. It's humid, there's no air conditioning, and frogs croak in chorus outside.

After what seems like an age and another ring on the bell, a slightly decrepit little woman appears, her silver hair in big rollers with a blue hair net and matching house coat. She's tired. It's 1am. She looks over the rims of her pointy pink reading glasses and takes in the situation, the young mother and sleeping kid. *Is she on the run?*

She speaks in a crackly southern accent with a bleaty sheep tone. 'I'm Mavis, the manager. Can I help you? It's awfully late to be checkin' in, honey.'

'I really need a room for my daughter and me. Sorry it's so late.'

'What y'all say honey, I can't understand ya? Mavis looks puzzled. 'Where y'all from, England or someplace?'

Gala is exhausted and really over being foreign and

misunderstood. She speaks louder and more slowly, 'I need a room please. I am from New Zealand.'

Mavis looks puzzled and chews on her pencil, flicking through her register. 'Never heard of the place. Is that in Europe? Well, I got a double I can let you have for sixteen dollars. Check out is 11am.'

'That'll do, thanks.' Gala sighs out and pulls twenty bucks from her leather shoulder bag.

Mavis comes out from behind the counter armed with a huge jangling copper key ring. She's barely four-foot-tall and walks with a limp down the slippery broken path to the room. Gala follows and nearly squashes a little brown frog on the path. They're all over the place.

Mavis opens the door to number twenty-three. The pink, fluorescent motel sign flickers a surreal light over the tiny room. Gala takes in the double bed, which looks good after a three-day solid bus trip.

'Thanks, Ma'am, this will be fine.'

Mavis, waves her skinny arm, jingling her collection of brass and coloured bangles in the direction of the swamp cooler. 'There's a swamp cooler if y'all too hot in here.'

She totters over and flicks the switch and the dusty swamp cooler kicks into life with a heavy drone. The cool swampy air fills the room. 'TV works, no cable, only local channels.' She flicks the old television on. 'Need anything special for the kid? Y'all need a cot or somethin?'

Gala shakes her head. She really just wants the little woman to leave. 'No thanks, we'll be fine.'

Mavis hands the key to Gala. 'All righty then. Good night, honey.'

Gala hears the jingling keys disappear down the pathway.

With the chorus of the frogs and crickets outside, the drone from the cooler just brings in the bass. She closes the door quietly and pulls the chain lock into place. Leah has snuggled into the middle of the sagging double bed with the pink candlewick bedspread and matching satin pillows. Gala smiles, watching her sleeping daughter curled up like a kitten with a pink neon light-halo. She can't stop thinking about her husband, coming home and finding them gone. *What have I done, what the fuck have I done?* Gala lets the sadness come over her, wash over her, pull at her insides, ache. She stands, slowly pulling off her jacket. Tears well up like warm relief as she snuggles next to her sleeping child. *Dam that TV is still on.* Too tired and sad to get up to turn it off, Gala falls asleep as a Texan car salesman shows off his latest line of brand-new Cadillacs.

Los Angeles to Denton Greyhound Ride, 1975

Gala looks out of the Greyhound as it passes through Blithe, California, a town where old widows go to live out their last days in trailer homes. She and Leah have been on the bus for hours. The air conditioner is cranking and Gala wraps up in her denim jacket.

Across the aisle, a girl in her twenties, dressed like a cowgirl, with a red bandana and faded leather jacket, takes off her Ray-bans and smiles at Gala. 'Hi.'

'Hullo,' says Gala,

'You have an accent.'

'Yes, I'm from Auckland, New Zealand.'

'Oh. I hear it's beautiful over there.' The girl looks interested.

'It is. Where are you going?'

'Back home to Arizona. We should be getting in sometime tomorrow, early.'

'Tomorrow?' Gala is panicking. 'I thought we get into Texas around midnight.'

The cowgirl laughs, 'Midnight? Midnight in about three days. It's a long ride to Texas, baby. Haven't you ever been there?' She says *baby*, like Janis Joplin.

Gala's still in shock. 'No I'm going to see a friend there. I had no idea how far it was, really. I had to get away. Three days, God! That's a long ride all right.'

She cuddles Leah, looking down at her blonde curls, holding back the tears. Her stomach gets tight, partly because she hasn't eaten all day but mostly because of the gut-wrenching fear of what she's done. *What was she thinking?* She didn't even check how far it was after the last stop, where she ordered pancakes for Leah and just a coffee for herself, to save their last dollars. They were down to thirty-six bucks.

Tracy and Tad, Southfork Trailer Park, 1975

While checking out, Gala and her hungry daughter get directions from Mavis to the nearest available coffee and donuts. Loaded up with a coffee and a huge plain-glazed, Gala attempts to call her only contact in Texas, Janet the Planet. She'd tried calling a few times during the bus trip, but nobody answered. The hot morning sun is firing up for a scorcher and it's steamy inside the grubby phone booth. Leah, perched on the suitcase, is devouring a huge sugar

TELEPHONE

sprinkled Winchell's. She's come alive after the long journey and a shower. All country girl in flared blue jeans, white t-shirt and a straw hat. She listens to her mother on the phone.

'Oh, so Janet and her sister are both in Aspen? Skiing? Okay. When will they be back? Oh. Okay. A friend of Janet's, yes thanks, I'll get that number. Her name's Tracy. Okay, thanks again.'

Gala dials.

After another donut and more time waiting in the killing sun, a beat-up yellow Combie van hoons up to the phone booth. Gala and Leah are showered in warm dust. Heavy metal's blasting out and a skinny ginger-haired hippy-chick with freckles and a cheeky grin leans out.

'Hey, you Gala? I'm Tracy and this here's Cindy.' A little blonde head pops up, grinning. 'I said get in back Cindy, right now!'

Tracy's tone is sharp and Leah looks up at her mum. But she's too busy loading everything into the van to notice.

Gala mumbles gratitude as she swings up front with her new friend.

Tracy cranks up the van, with a shudder and speeds off, dust flying.

'So how y'all know Janet and Susan?' she yells out over the engine and a Deep Purple song.

'Oh, we were hanging out in Auckland, nightclubs and stuff. We knew the same musicians and crowd, you know. They're a lot of fun, eh?'

Tracy lights up a Marlboro non-filter and takes a long drag. 'Yep, them rich bitches sure know how to party all right. *Smoke on the Water, don don, don, da don da don,* don't you love this song?'

TRACE

Tracy's singing out of tune with great gusto. The van fills up with smoke. The two little girls are bouncing to the music on the mattress in the back, squealing with pure joy.

'Shut up you two and sit your butts down, or we'll have to drop y'all off someplace!' Tracy laughs, her tone is sharper. She is on a roll, 'Well, I live in the Southfork Trailer Park, south of town. When Mama died, she left me and my brother her trailer. It's not much. Tad lives there part-time until he pisses me off and I kick him out for a bit.' She takes a long drag and grins at Gala. 'There's the fucking guy right there.'

The Combie pulls up next to a rusty trailer home. A tall, grubby, good-looking Texan with a beard stands in the doorway.

'Who's this y'all brang home? Y'know we don't got much room, Trace.'

Tracy's cheerful demeanour darkens. 'Now that's a friendly Southern welcome, Tad. Sheeit, you could melt ice with that kinda hospitality. This here's Gala and she's from New Zealand. Friend of Janet Sanders, *and* she plays the guitar so why don't ya find your manners and get us both a Bud? Lazy son of a bitch, what did *you* do today? Get a job?'

Tad ignores her and goes inside the trailer. He comes out with a beer and hands the frosty can to Gala. It's a godsend in the sticky Denton heat.

Between gulps Gala says, 'Thanks. I was really thirsty, not really used to these temperatures.'

'What'd she say?' Tad calls out to his sister, 'I can't understand her accent.'

Tracy rolls her eyes at Gala. 'She's from New Zeeeealand dummy. They speak Australian.'

Gala listens as the brother and sister bicker about her like she isn't there. She pans the inside of the claustrophobic trailer, deciding that the pair probably don't subscribe to 'Trailer Homes and Gardening'. The dirty grey-white shag rug had seen better days. Green rubbish bags full of empty Bud cans lie around and ashtrays overflow on the grimy coffee table. Tad sinks back into his spot on the worn lazy boy and resumes watching Dukes of Hazzard.

'Hey, you lazy asshole, why didn't y'all get me a beer?' Tracy lights up another Marlboro.

Tad turns up the TV volume, drowning his sister out.

Gala wonders what she's in for and looks around for somewhere safe to put her belongings. The two little girls are giggling in the bedroom.

'Throw your stuff in that cupboard, honey. Tad, you could've helped our guest get settled in instead of watching that dumb show. It's a re-run anyways.'

'No, it ain't no re-run, Trace, and she ain't my guest neither. Leave me alone, bitch.'

'Oh, shut up ass-wipe, what's for dinner? Don't suppose ya bought any food did ya?' Tracy spat out to Gala. 'All he's good for is stacking up the fridge with cheap-ass beer, not much else. Doesn't lay a finger to help or nothin'. Mom would clip his ears good if she was alive.' She heads over to the crusty looking fridge. 'Let's see now. Poooweee. Somethin' up n' died in here Tad.'

'Must be that can of chili you left there Tracy. Don't go blaming me like you always do.'

Gala steers herself through the obstacle course of platform heels, piles of clothes and more overstuffed garbage bags, puts her things away in the cupboard while the pair bicker back and forth.

The night air brings some relief from the humid heat and, outside on the deck, a domestic trailer park scene is in progress. Tad has stripped down to a sweat-stained Harley Davidson tank-top and is lighting the BBQ, smoking a cigar and muttering. 'Yeah, the bitch roped me into fixin' supper.'

Tracy's yelling out through the bathroom window, 'Clean that grill off good, Tad. How long since you used it? When you cooked them T-Bones - weeks ago wasn't it? What a fuckin' loser.'

Gala goes over to Tad who is scraping the heck out of the grill. 'Is there anything I can do to help?'

Tad slides his cigar round as he yells back to Tracy,

'What'd she say?'

'She's talkin' to me, dummy. Just cook our steaks and mind your own beeswax.'

Tracy replies rather formally to Gala, 'Well, honey, you could find some plates and silverware if you like. Might have to wash some. Tad never cleans up after his lazy self.'

Gala heads to the kitchen. The counter is strewn with empty cans of mouldy chili, more overflowing ashtrays and half a bottle of Jack Daniels. Doesn't look like anyone has cleaned up in a long while. Tracy comes in from the bedroom. She's changed into some super short jean shorts and a black tube top. The two girls are playing with Barbies on the couch.

Tracy adopts a more friendly tone, watching Gala washing off some plates. 'Do you like hard liquor, honey?'

'Well sometimes.' Gala says shyly.

'We got a live one here, Tad,' Tracy calls out, then to Gala in her best Southern hospitality voice, 'Well me and my brother

HARLEY
DAVIDSON

like a shot of JD around sunset. Helps take the edge off. Care to join us?'

She pulls three shot glasses from out of her fat patchworked purse. Ruby's Café is written on the shiny glass.

'Where'd you steal those beauties?' Tad's smile shows he'd be handsome if he brushed his teeth once in a while. They really are cigar-stained.

'Mind your own business Tad, want her thinkin' we lowlifes?'

She hands a full shot glass to Gala. 'Here, Sugar, knock this back. It'll help. Trust me.'

Gala downs the strong dark liquor and offers her glass back up to Tracy.

'Hey now, Tad, what'd I tell ya?'

Gala settles out on the deck watching the magnificent orange-red sun go down. The girls chase each other around a broken-down black Ranchero. The steaks smell divine with hickory smoke and garlic. She relaxes into a daydream.

Crypt Night Club, Queen Street, Auckland, 1970

In the dark interior cave-like space, a local underground band, The Brew, are storming through their last set, acid-jazz with a dash of funk, alto-sax is soaring high-crescendo through the solo. The band is tight. Gala, Aida and two Texan girls dance together, feeling the band's pulse and grooving to it. Janet is a smoking redhead in hip-rider blue jeans and a satin blue low-cut top with loads of Indian bead necklaces and bangles. Three laidback-cool US sailors, in uniform (girls love a man in uniform) are watching their moves.

'Hey Gala, these guys are pretty cute, huh?' Janet winks at her.

LOVE
1970

'Yeah, pretty cute. Look like trouble though.'

Janet whispers in her sister Susan's ear, 'fancy some trouble, sis?'

'Sure, why not. I'd fancy hangin' with some brothers from our country.'

Together like double trouble, the two Texan babes sidle up to the guys and begin their flirtatious southern chit-chat. Gala stays on the dance floor with Aida, a tall Gauguin-like Maori girl in her twenties, long blue-ebony hair swaying with her slow sensuous moves.

Susan rushes over to the girls, 'Hey, they've got some gear. By the way, the cute black guy, Jay, hands off, baby, he's all mine. Yeah, they're here for R n' R, last stop, Bangkok.' She's giggling, excited, 'hey I'd like to bang some cock and do some gear for that matter.'

Aida follows Susan's swagger back to the booth. Gala watches her go and turns to the stage, focusing on her man, Billy, the handsome sandy-haired sax player in his thirties, blowing a cool solo over a James Brown groove. She waits until he finishes the solo and joins the girls, now all focused on Jay, who's spinning a tale or two about the East.

'I've got to go soon Janet,' she says quietly, 'Billy gets off at 2 am.'

'Yeah, I hope to get off soon too Babe. Here take some of this and try it,' then quietly, 'in the bathroom.' She presses a folded dollar bill into Gala's palm.

Inside the sterile cubicle, Gala cuts a line of pure heroin with a nail file on top of her patent leather purse. She snorts it using the American dollar bill, waits a beat then does another line for good measure.

The band is on its last song, Foxy Lady, as the drug kicks

in. Gala sways as she tries to open the toilet door. The whole bathroom is swirling as she holds on to the walls, slowly making her way back to the table. The singer thanks the people left in the club and harsh lights come on. Gala is nodding out in the booth, propped up between Janet and smooth-talking Jay, who's still telling tales. He leans into Janet with his heavy-lidded eyes, 'Hey, baby, not too cool having your girl dying over here.'

'I know, she's a novice. Shit, here comes Billy.'

Billy takes one look at his spaced-out girlfriend, with her eyes rolling back, 'Jesús, baby, what happened to you?'

'Oh, she's had too much to drink, those Tequila Sunrises, they sure pack a punch, huh?' Janet covers with the speed of a lying teenager.

Gala tries to focus as Billy helps her up and guides her up the stairs to the Queen Street exit. He waits as she throws up on the street then puts her in the passenger seat of his red Austin mini.

'That's so fucking embarrassing, you getting so out of it at the club. That's my workplace, you stupid bitch! Jesus Christ, Gala! '

Gala's mascara is running. Her face is pale. 'I'm sorry Billy, they were too strong those drinks.'

'Fuck, it's like you're on drugs or something.' He takes her face and looks into her eyes close up, then slaps her across the face. Gala crumples in the seat, crying.

Ruby's Café, Denton, Texas, 1975

Gala wakes up in the piercing sun on the deck of the trailer, with a Mexican blanket and a hangover. She panics and looks for Leah inside. She's curled up with Cindy on the couch. TV is still on, cartoons droning. Cicadas start screeching with the sunrise. It's already hot and sticky. Gala rummages for clean clothes in her suitcase and drags out blue jeans and a white shirt. She finds the shower. Tad and Tracy are still sleeping. She showers and towel dries her hair on the deck, the sun feels good on her washed skin. She puts on some plum lipstick and smells bacon sizzling on the stove. Tad looks up from the pan,

'Where you off to, girl? You're looking pretty this mornin'.' He has some Southern charm all right.

Gala blushes with the compliment. She replies slowly and clearly. 'Oh, I have to find work in town. I've run out of money'.

Tad's green eyes light up. 'What kinda work ya lookin' for?'

'Waitressing. I had a good job back in LA, made around a hundred in tips a shift, food and cocktails.'

Tad smiles. 'Hey now, that sounds pretty good. I could take you over to Ruby's. They need help sometimes, especially round July fourth.'

'Thanks that would be very helpful, Tad.'

'We can get going after we eat. Tracy won't be up for hours. She watches the tube till 3am most nights. Y'all want some bacon and hashbrowns?'

Gala gratefully takes the plate Tad offers and watches him serve up the steaming vittles while still managing to keep his big cigar in place. The crispy-sweet hickory bacon is perfect and the coffee he pours her is strong and black. Perfect for a hangover.

Soon they're speeding into town in Tad's black 1960 Cadillac, with the two little 'best friends' in the backseat. The red vinyl interior is spotless, huge contrast to the trailer interior. Tad's tanned hunky arm is out the window. He's relaxed, smoking his cigar with his Formula One sunglasses on, hair blowing back. He slaps the side of the car.

'I was going to sell this baby to raise some cash a while back. Changed my mind when someone actually wanted to buy her. Love this ol' girl.'

He kicks her into top gear and speeds through the cornfields. Gala thinks they're as yellow as Van Gogh's sunflowers as they flash by. Tad is definitely in charge. He clicks on the radio and the howlingest blues track comes on. 'The Sky is Crying' by Elmore James fills up the Caddy with its rich soul. Gala relaxes and smiles, the sun warming her face.

'This here's my favourite Dallas station, you get some sweet-ass tunes on this show. Great guitar players in Dallas. Man listen to this playing.'

The sky is crying, can you see the tears roll down the street?

Tad lights up a new cigar and slides the Caddy into the curb opposite a rustic biker bar.

'Ruby's is right across the street. I'll drop you off here. Got kicked outta there last week. Guess I had a little too much bourbon, sheeitt. Yeah, some skinny bitch tryin' to tell me I gave her the clap or somethin'. Didn't even know that whore. Didn't really mean to hit her, she just pissed me right off. Hey now, good luck, girl. I'll take these two rascals to the playground down the street.'

Tad pulls away from the curb with the two girls giggling in the back.

The entrance to Ruby's Café is swampy, lined with ferns and whiskey barrels and huge logs of redwood surround the deck. The front door is dark hand-adzed wood. Gala straightens her white shirt and uses her shoulder to push the heavy door ajar. The room is dank, smelling of cigar smoke and humming with the drone of swamp coolers. Once Gala's eyes adjust to the inside light, she makes out a rustic bar. Half a dozen long-haired Texans, all wearing cowboy hats, are knocking back Lone Star Longnecks and Budweisers. Above their heads, Cuban cigar smoke is forming hazy clouds.

Gala notices the balding 'Elvis' bartender, decked out in a shiny red cowboy shirt and serious sideburns. He's pouring a long cold one from the tap and winks at her as she approaches the well-worn counter.

'Howdy, what can I get for you, girl?'

'Hullo, I was wondering if you had any work, Sir?' Gala blushed as all the cowboys turn to check her out.

'Well what kinda work y'all looking for, Miss? It is Miss, right? I don't see no ring on your finger, honey.'

'Well, I have experience in waitressing.' Gala wishes she'd worn her wedding ring, but she'd left it back in LA with her goodbye note.

'I always need extra help around the fourth. If you work out, I'll keep you on. How old are you?'

'Twenty-four, Sir.'

'I'm gonna need to see some ID, Miss.'

Gala hands over her Green Card.

'Uh oh, we got ourselves an alien here, boys.' The chuckle from the cowboys ripples down the length of the bar. 'That all checks out, Miss Gala.' Elvis hands back the card. And in a kinder tone, 'Come in and train tomorrow afternoon, round three. Fill out this application and bring it on in with you.' He winks at her with a grin.

'Thanks, I'll be here at three.'

Gala smiles shyly, takes the form and walks back out to the exit. She leans into the thick wooden door to push it open to the street. In the stream of sunlight, she looks down and sees a black dusty cowboy boot. She gazes up to the face of a tall Mexican heartbreaker who's helping her with the door.

'Here, Baby, I'll help you. It's heavy,'

'Thanks.' Gala is quite taken by his rugged handsome face and muscular arms.

'Don't pay no mind to those ignorant crackers, girl. Come down and talk to me after I finish tonight, and I'll fill you in on this dump.'

'Oh, you work here?'

He extends a warm brown hand and shakes Gala's hand. She likes the wide turquoise and silver bracelet on his wrist. 'Johnny Magana from the Dallas Rhythm Aces. I'm the lead guitarist. We're the house band and pretty much rock this place. Liven it up, you know.' His smile is contagious. 'Do you like the blues? Do y'all like Johnny Winter?'

'Yes,' Gala lights up, 'I have his first album.'

'Well, he and his brother Edgar play here sometimes. They grew up in Texas. Janis Joplin did too. She played here before she left and hit the big time. What's your name, honey?'

'Gala, and I love Janis,' she says shyly.

'Well, you talk real nice, Miss Gala. Hope I see you tonight?'

Johnny turns and strides into the shadows of the bar then to the stage. His long shiny black hair is braided at the back and the white tank top shows off his muscular arms. The faded blue jeans fit perfectly, set off by a low-slung black leather belt.

Gala heads on to the street, breathless, thinking she's never ever seen such a gorgeous man. Standing on the corner she hears a smooth blues guitar start up and a low rich voice sing, 'I say one day, woman, you're gonna want me like I want you.'

The soulful sound goes through Gala as she waits for the lights to change. She wants to see Johnny play the blues tonight more than anything. Crossing the street, she looks out for Tad's car and walks to the playground. The weedy overgrown play area is deserted. No sign of the girls. Gala panics, running around the playground like a disturbed mother hen, calling out for her daughter. What was she thinking, she'd only known Tad for a day or so?

'Mummy, Mummy,' Leah is running towards her mother with a huge chocolate ice-cream cone. 'Look Mummy, Tad says they make the biggest ice-creams in Texas, you want some?' Leah pushes the dripping cone into Gala's mouth as she leans down to hug her.

Gala laughs with relief and holds her lovely child tightly.

Tad's smoking another stogy and revs up the engine as they approach. The afternoon sun warms them as they slide into the purring beast. Tad has the top down and turns to Gala. 'Y'all right? Looks like you bin cryin,' girl. Didn't those shitheads hire you?'

'No, I just couldn't find the kids. I got a fright.' Gala says quietly, appreciating his concern.

'I said I'd watch them, girl. Took them down to Dairy Queen to get ice-cream.'

The two girls are in the back seat, faces covered in chocolate and giggling. They look like they've been having fun all right. Tad seems more relaxed with kids than his sister.

Gala turns to Tad. 'I think I did all right at Ruby's. They want me to come in tomorrow and train. Said they'll hire me if it works out. I hope I can do it. Things are really different down here. You all talk so slowly.'

'Don't worry, honey. They gonna tease you though, cos ya talk funny, ya do, real quick and mumbled-like. Stand up for yourself. Give it right back to them. They'll like ya and respect ya too.' Tad smiles at her.

'I'll do my best. I need the money. Thanks for watching the kids, Tad.'

He doesn't reply, just blows smoke rings as the Caddy slows at the traffic lights.

'Move ya black ass, porch monkey,' he yells out the window, as a young black teenager makes his way over the cross walk. Then to Gala, 'I hate the way those goddam niggers move slow

on purpose when ya slow for the light. Pisses me right off. Good thing I don't got my rifle with me. He's lucky I don't got my gun!' Tad is loud enough for the teenager to hear. He walks quicker with his head down.

Tad guns the Caddy at the green light and throws his head back. 'Hoooweeee, I scared that boy good. Ya see that? Ya see that Sambo run!'

Gala slinks down in the seat, cringing and thinking, *if you are an uneducated grown man, living in your dead mother's trailer, wearing the same underwear for days, no job and drinking and fighting with your train-wreck sister every night, maybe picking on somebody you consider to be worse off, has some reward.* She is shocked, never having heard such a racist rant before. She doesn't know what to say, so she decides to keep her mouth closed. Tad cranks up the car radio and another sweet southern blues riff fills up the silence. Gala closes her eyes and daydreams.

3am Ponsonby Villa, New Zealand, 1970

Gala is sleeping. Billy enters the room and wakes her. His tie is askew and he's slurring his words. 'Here baby try this.' He presses a tab of acid into Gala's mouth. 'This is Rianne. Isn't she cute? She wanted to meet you.'

Billy starts taking his tie off. Rianne, barely seventeen, stands awkwardly at the doorway. She's tipsy, shy with bright red lips and a crumpled maxi-dress, unsure what to do. Gala gets up naked, grabs some clothes, and dresses as she heads to the toilet. She walks back past the bedroom and looks at Rianne for a moment then takes off down the front steps, past the sax case and granny shoes strewn in the doorway. She pulls on her denim jacket. The early morning Ponsonby mist spreads out like dusky clouds.

'That's the last time, Billy. The last bloody time,' Gala yells back at the house.

She walks quickly, buckling up her leather ankle straps as she goes up Summer Street to Ponsonby Road. Birds are waking up and she's crying. The acid starts to come on: fluorescent effect, over sepia, surreal trees are glowing-red-energy. She passes the dairy and the second-hand shops, which appear stylised like illustrations. Gala swerves down the road and opens a small wooden gate into a duplex. She carefully enters the darkened bedroom.

'Janet, wake up. Please. I need to talk to you.'

'What's the fucking time? Gala, what's the matter?'

Janet pulls on a robe and drapes a patchwork quilt over her sleeping dark haired lover. With her finger to her lips to quieten Gala, the girls walk quietly into the kitchen. Janet puts the kettle on for a cuppa. Gala is tripping and crying.

'It's the last time he's fucking around with another girl. This one's even younger than me. He brought her home to share. Bastard. I'm so sick of it. You know what else, I think I'm pregnant.' She cries into Janet's arms.

'Shit, baby, better knock off the partying then, know what I mean?'

Janet holds her friend. Gala nods, sobbing into her embrace. Janet wipes her face with a tissue.

'I'm heading down to Texas soon with Sue. Charlie's coming too. You're always welcome at my folks' place in Denton. We'll show you a good time in my hometown.'

The sun comes up through the kitchen window.

The Dallas Rhythm Aces play Ruby's Café, 1975

Inside the trailer, Tracy is toasting a grape pop tart, pouring coffee and smoking a menthol all at the same time.

'Yeah, I heard about them Rhythm Aces. They tear it up on the blues, girl. You like that lead guitarist huh? Gotta watch out for those Mexican wetbacks though, honey. They crazy motherfuckers.'

The fake mauve jam is dripping into Tracy's mouth as she talks, the menthol smoke swirling around her. 'Shoot, we'll make the bed up in back of the van. Cindy's used to me going to Ruby's. She just crashes out and I check on her from time to time.' Trace seems to have all the experience of a partying van mother. 'Y'all want a pop-tart?'

'No thanks.' Gala isn't too sure what they are made of.

'Hey, Gala, that orange mini dress of yours fits me puurrfect. I'd sure like to wear it tonight.'

Gala sees that her suitcase is open with all her clothes strewn over the couch and realizes that Tracy has been right through it, trying everything on. *Different ways down here,* she thinks.

'Oh, Okay.'

'How do ya like these shoes with it?'

Tracy's holding up the tallest silver platform shoes. 'These will look so cute with that dress. I feel so tall in these. Don't you just love them?' She wipes the remains of the pop-tart on her Daisy Dukes and holds up Gala's new mini dress, turning slowly and admiring herself in the greasy full-length mirror. Gala looks in disbelief as her dress is adopted but is too polite to object, being from New Zealand and a guest in Tracy's home. She'd hardly worn it.

Tracy spins around from the mirror. 'Cindy, you bring that dress back right now or I'll tan your hide!'

Cindy is jumping on the double bed in Leah's full-length cotton dress. Tracy grabs her and smacks her backside. Cindy wriggles away and crawls under the bed.

Tracy's speaks in a sharp tone, 'I said give me that dress back, you little brat, or you'll be sorry. I'll sic Uncle Tad on you girl.'

Cindy's sticky fist is protruding from under the bed, 'No Mama, here it is.'

'Don't you know it's bad manners to take someone's stuff

without asking?'

It's quiet under the bed and then Cindy crawls out naked and runs to the bathroom. Leah laughs out loud at the sight of her little bare bum and the tension is broken.

Tracy is back to trying on clothes and preparing for the night out. She finally settles back on Gala's dress and paints her nails silver to match her shoes. Gala changes into a white cotton embroidered blouse she bought in East LA and her favourite blue jeans. The children take a bath and play with Barbies while Tracy fixes supper. She serves up macaroni and cheese, boasting that she made it from scratch. Gala notices the Chef Boy R Dee package mix in the trash but decides not to argue with the 'chef.' Again, she's too polite and now a little afraid of her southern hostess.

The amber sun is going down on the endless Texas horizon as the two young mothers cruise to Ruby's in Tracy's rattling Combie van. She's got ZZ Top blasting out full volume and is singing out of tune, also at full volume. She parks in the alley at the side of the bar. The little girls start whining to come in for a soda.

'We'll git you something if you're good. Now quit your whining both of you. Get back into bed and go to sleep. It's way past ten o'clock!'

Tracy's definitely a no-frills-no-nonsense kinda mother and apparently also untruthful. Gala checks her watch and sees it's just nine but decides not to correct her. She tucks the girls in and tries not to feel too guilty.

'Don't worry, we'll check on 'em,' Tracy reassures her as she locks the van.

The call of Johnny's guitar has Gala floating to the entrance. It pulls at her core. It's the most soulful sound she's ever known.

The beefy cowboy bouncer checks their IDs. 'Okay, go right in. Ladies are free tonight.' He winks at Gala as he pushes the door open.

Gala doesn't notice, just focuses on where the sound is coming from, and makes her way towards the dark red glow of the stage. She passes Tracy, already in a clinch with some sweaty dude, his tongue right down her throat. Gala sees Johnny's black leather hat to the side of the stage. He's wearing a black western shirt that accentuates his broad shoulders, black jeans and those same smooth boots. She feels weak at the knees. He's not showing off either, hanging back, with the singer taking the spotlight. Gala sways gently to the groove, seduced by the sweet emotion of the guitar. The Rhythm Aces kick into a Johnny Winter blues: Be Careful with a Fool. In the solo, the singer stands back and gives Johnny the spotlight. He plays a strong, soaring solo, enjoying the attention from the rowdy fans, whistling and hooting for more. Waitresses are bringing pitchers of beer to the stage.

Gala finds a table and waits nervously for her rock star guitar man. The set finishes and he walks over to her smiling.

'So, you made it, Miss Gala.'

'Yes, I'm glad I did. Wow your band is great and you're an excellent guitarist!'

'Hey now, don't flatter me, it'll go to my head. What do y'all want to drink?'

Gala is quite overwhelmed by his attention and up close he's even sexier with his powerful arms glowing from playing.

'I'll take a beer thanks.' She smiles shyly.

'What brand do you like? Don't think they've got any Australian beer here.' He winks at her.

'Actually, it's New Zealand, separate to Aussie. A Heineken

will be lovely thanks.'

Johnny soon returns and places the frosty beer on a coaster in front of her. 'I'm glad you like my band. We dig the blues. I got into that last song when I saw you there dancing.'

Gala, almost swooning, sips her beer.

'Now watch these girls working, Gala. See that one, Lydia, she's been working here for years and never puts up with any bullshit from these crackers.'

Gala studies Lydia, a tanned amazon, making her way through the crowd, serving drinks, taking orders, giving change and having a laugh with customers. She makes it all look so easy.

Tracy plonks herself down at the table and grabs a napkin to wipe her face. 'I can't get rid of that horny son of a bitch. Say now, who's your friend? Aren't ya going to introduce us?'

'Tracy this is Johnny Magana,' Gala reluctantly says.

'Hellooo Johnny. Hola,' she giggles, and makes goo goo eyes at him. 'Man, you sure are a sexy babe.'

'Well thanks Tracy,' Johnny chuckles. 'What are you drinking?'

'Harvey Wallbanger? Make it a double thanks, lover.'

She squeezes Johnny's bum as he gets up. Gala is annoyed and uncomfortable with Tracy's flirtatious antics. Lover? That was a bit much.

'Well, you scored yourself a real cutie. Damn he's fine. Bet he's a real studmuffin, a real stick man. Mmmm Mmmmm.' Tracy takes a long sip of her drink.

'Tracy, Johnny and I are discussing my new job here and I'd like to finish that conversation, if you don't mind.' Gala is surprised by her own emotion.

'Damn, well you don't have to go and get all shitty girl! I

know when I'm not wanted. I'll go get a cute piece of ass for myself. Watch me.' Tracy grabs the colourful Wallbanger complete with pink umbrella, out of Johnny's hand, and wiggles off in her tall platforms.

'What's her problem?' Johnny asks, amused by the back view of Tracy swaying, with her drink in hand.

'I don't know.' Gala is embarrassed.

'Your friend is a character.' Johnny grins at her.

'Well to be honest she's a friend of my friend Janet. I just met her yesterday.' Gala glances at Johnny's eyes, hypnotic aqua-blue, as they sip their beers.

'The boys are heading back up on stage. I better go. Y'all sticking around Gala?'

'I'm staying until the end,' *of time,* she wants to add.

Johnny looks pleased. 'Okay, beautiful, see you soon.'

Johnny leans across the table and kisses Gala lightly on the mouth. Smooth as a jaguar, he's moving through the crowd. On stage, he picks up his black Stratocaster and the band kicks into a slow blues. Gala is still frozen like a doll in a dollhouse, savouring the kiss on her lips, not wanting to sip her beer in case it disappears. Tracy is right up front by the stage, gyrating in slow sexy moves, right in front of Johnny. It looks like she's had more than alcohol, the way she's swaying and wobbling on her high platforms. Gala closes her eyes, listening to the music, and lets it take her like a lover, floating in a sweet blue dream, still tasting his kiss.

'My God, I have to check on the kids,' she says out loud.

She practically runs out of the bar and heads for the van. The two girls are curled up together on the bed, sleeping like angels. Gala kisses Leah on the forehead and says a prayer as she closes the van door. She passes a drunken cowboy vomiting in the alley and pushes open Ruby's door. Up onstage, Tracy's managed to grab a microphone. The burly bouncer is dragging her off stage but she's clinging hard to the mic.

'Play some heavy metal y'all. Yeeeeeooowww! I'm sick of this slow blues shit!' Tracy spots Gala in the crowd. 'Where y'all bin, kiwi-girl? I sang with the band. Rocked the house, baby!' She's gesticulating wildly as the determined bouncer drags her and her tall heels off the stage.

Gala is embarrassed and makes her way to the stage, beckoning Johnny over.

'I'm sorry Johnny, I'll have to get going. Tracy's really out of it.'

'Yeah, she was hard to miss up here. What are you doing later, mija?'

'Nothing really.'

'I'll come by after we finish. Is that too late? We can go down to the Lewisville Lake.' He looks earnest.

'Okay,' she says, smiling up at his handsome face. 'Do you know where the Southfork Trailer Park is?'

'I've lived in this town for ten years, kid. I know where everything is. Drive safe now.'

Tracy's crashed out with her head hanging out the window. Gala is driving the Combie with care, focusing in front, staying next to the white line and remembering which side to drive on, the right, the opposite of New Zealand. No streetlights on the road to Southfork Denton, only the light of the giant full moon. The frogs are chorusing up a storm in the eerie swampland. A black Labrador runs out barking as she pulls into the trailer park driveway. Blue light shines out from Tracy's living room.

Tad's up watching TV. He strides out, smoking.

'What's up with Trace? She get hammered as per usual?'

'Yeah, you could say that. Help me with her Tad.'

Tad swings down from the deck and pulls his rag-doll sister out of the van, muttering. 'Yeah, bitch always gets fucked up at Ruby's.'

Tad staggers inside the trailer and dumps Tracy in the bedroom. Gala and Tad carry the girls inside and tuck them up on the couch. Amazingly, they stay asleep.

Tad pours a shot of Jack Daniels for himself and hands one to Gala. She takes it out to the deck and looks up at the full moon, marvelling how it's upside down, a totally different sight than the New Zealand view. She gets her guitar and sits down on an old leather car seat to wait for Johnny. She knocks back the smooth whiskey and starts finger picking, the notes blending with the frog chorus. Thinking of a new song, just letting the words fall out, singing shyly about her new love.

I saw you coming, from a long way away
You were riding on a stallion
It was a dusty day

Around 2am the shiny black hood of a Mustang noses into the driveway. Johnny climbs out from the black leather seat and smiles up at Gala, who's managed to stay awake.

'Hi, beautiful girl, where is everyone?'

'They've crashed out, Tad's watching TV. He's Tracy's brother.'

Johnny swings up on the deck with all the ease of an athlete.

Gala is melting with his closeness. He checks out Gala's guitar. 'Hey, babe, I didn't know you played guitar, far out. Can you play me something?'

Gala finds his hypnotic smile irresistible. 'Well, I wrote a blues, Mabel's Blues. Want to hear that?'

Johnny nods and smiles down at her.

She sings the A minor blues, closing her eyes and really feeling the lyrics.

Talking in your sleep, Mama, what have you got to hide?
Talking halfway through the night, lord knows you can't be
satisfied

As she finishes, Johnny is enthusiastic. 'Hey, I like that song, you *can* sing the blues, girl.'

Gala jumps up, flattered with the compliment. Her cheeks are burning. 'Thanks Johnny, would you like a beer?'

'Nah, I'm good. Think I have everything I need right here

with that big ol' moon and you.'

He takes her in his arms and kisses her gently, longer than the first one. Gala feels the warmth of his muscular arms wrapped around her and responds to his delicious kiss. 'Come and sit with me, baby. Let me look at you in this light. See how the moon turns everything silver. It's like right now you and I are the only people left on this planet. I mean did you ever see such a full moon?'

Gala cannot speak at first, overwhelmed by his delicious warmth and smell, Jovan Musk, she suspects. 'It's beautiful and looks different in this part of the world. Different shadows. See the woman singing in the moon, Johnny?'

Johnny laughs and tries to make out the shape. 'You make me laugh. *La Luna*, the moon in Spanish. Hey, I brought something for you.' He reaches into his jeans pocket and pulls out a small silver cigarette case, flicks it open and pulls out a perfectly rolled joint.

'Goodness, you American guys are pretty smooth. Nice cigarette case.'

'Do you smoke, honey?'

'Sometimes.'

'Well, this is some strong Jamaican blend my brother gave me. You don't need a lot to get high.' He chuckles as he lights up.

Inhaling a long drag he hands it to Gala who takes it gingerly. She takes a long toke and starts coughing. Johnny's laughing, throwing back his long mane of jet-black hair and letting out a full stream of smoke.

'Don't worry, baby, I've seen experienced stoners have the same reaction to this bud. It's strong. My bro calls it the Marley. Just take it slow, little tokes at first.'

Gala tries the joint again, little tokes, and holds the smoke in. Smiling, she lets the smoke out slowly feeling the warm buzz come over her.

'I'm glad you came out here to see me, Johnny.'

Johnny surrounds Gala and kisses her fully on the mouth. She melts into him, closing her eyes and drinking in his warm male fragrance.

'I was looking forward to it all night. Couldn't wait for that last song to end. Hey, you wanna go down to the lake now?'

'Oh, okay,' Gala says slowly.

Johnny jumps off the deck and catches Gala as she follows, entranced. They drive down the dirt road. Gala leans back into the soft leather seat and watches Johnny handle the Mustang round the bends and turns. *Life is Hard*, a slow heartfelt Johnny Winter track plays as the moon follows them. Gala sees it all like a technicolor dream. Johnny parks and they follow the stream of moonlight through the birch trees. Johnny's thrown a Mexican blanket over his shoulder. Frogs are answering calls across the dark water. He strides to a spot and spreads the blanket out. Gala falls down next to him and they kiss. She's giving back to him now, offering herself. Johnny kisses her neck and gently opens up her blouse. She doesn't resist.

'I love your skin, girl. It's so soft,' he says quietly.

He kisses her shoulders. Gala opens his black shirt and can feel his heart beating under her gentle kisses. She wants to make love with this beautiful man but knows it's better to wait. She wants him for more than a one-night-stand.

'I think I should get back now. It's kinda late.'

'Okay, baby, just a few more minutes. I just want to hold you,' he whispers.

They watch the moonbeams dance off the rippling water.

Gala sits up and buttons up her blouse. Johnny's shirt is still open and she takes a glance at his chest, tanned and shining in the eerie light, driving back with Jimi Hendrix's *All Along the Watchtower* playing in the intoxicating sweet night air. One long kiss goodnight and Gala watches the Mustang disappear down the dusty road. She's way too excited to sleep.

Kitchen, Herne Bay, New Zealand, 1971

Billy's smoking a Pall Mall non-filter at the kitchen table. Gala's balancing a baby on her hip, stirring scrambled eggs, watching the toast and pouring a black coffee for Billy. He's hangover, smug, watching his woman working over the stove.

'Hey, babe, I can hold her for a bit.'

'Not while you're smoking, Billy.'

'Shit, don't be so uptight.'

It's quiet for a bit. The kitchen Phillips radio plays the Underdogs, *Sitting in the Rain*. Billy gets up from the table, grabs more coffee from the bench and starts pacing and smoking.

'I want you to come to the club tonight, want you to meet a couple of chicks from the show.'

'Why?'

'Well, these two are the foxiest out of all the dancers. You know, babe. The Tokyo Review, I'm playing at the Montmartre.'

Gala's emptying scrambled eggs onto the plates and buttering white toast. Baby Leah is gurgling in her baby seat on the kitchen table.

'So?'

Billy is disappointed at Gala's reaction. 'Shit, babe, where's the old spirit? I thought we could have some fun with them.

The show winds up Saturday night.'

Gala's tired and brushes her long brown hair back from her flushed face. 'Billy, I'm not into that orgy stuff anymore. Not with the baby around.'

'Shit, what's gotten into you Gala? You're no fun anymore.'

'I'm a mother now. You know, things change?'

Billy ignores her. 'Well, get your sister over tonight to babysit and wear something sexy, okay?

The Montmartre in Newmarket, a popular Auckland nightclub, has a charged atmosphere. Glamorous Japanese dancers are on stage, wearing white-beaded high-cut bikini bottoms with white high-feathered headdresses, their perfect natural breasts exposed. The band members are all in tuxedos, playing sexy R'n'B tunes. Gala is sitting at a table alone, watching the whole scene. The band guys are all ogling at the dancers, including Billy, who is soloing some smooth sax over a funky riff.

Later, back in their kitchen, Billy is in host mode, helping the taller Japanese girl, Yuko, smoke hash from two hot knives on the stove element. The other Japanese girl, Suzy, looks upset and jealous. She gets her bag and heads for the front door.

Yuko calls after her and they exchange intense words in Japanese.

'What's the matter? Why are you going?'

'Fuck this scene,' she replies. 'I'm not into drugs. They only seem interested in you anyway. I'm getting a taxi back to the hotel. Have fun, slut.'

She slams the front door. Yuko walks back down the hall to the kitchen and Gala watches the interaction with the two girls and then has a hit of hash. Billy is pleased with how it's all going. He's got the girl he wants after lining up the whole situation for three weeks and now it's all falling into place.

Gala and Yuko are drinking wine and laughing.

'Here I got this for you. A little gift from Tokyo.' Gala opens a package wrapped in pink tissue paper and pulls out a silk kimono with little flowers on it.

'I love it, thanks.' She tries it on over her outfit.

'We take bath together, OK?'

The girls are in the bath soaping each other and laughing. The bathroom has the soft light of vanilla candles with rose incense burning around the clawfoot bathtub. Billy watches from the doorway and smokes his Pall Mall.

'You two sure look pretty together. Two cultures, two different beauties.'

The girls laugh. They are high and ignore Billy's comments.

He tries hard to get in on the scene. 'I got you both some more wine,' leans over the bath, perving on the girls' shiny, soapy bodies topping up their glasses. 'Pity the goddamn bath's so goddamn small. I'd sure like to join you two honeys.'

The girls continue to ignore him.

Later in the bedroom, with a brass bed head and more candles, Yuko is above Gala, naked. Her long, black hair falls over Gala's small curvaceous body, stroking her thighs. She leans in and whispers to Gala. 'You tell husband, Yuko no like older man, only young girls or young boy, you tell, Okay?'

Gala sees Billy is in the doorway, watching the two girls make love. His face changes to a dark scowl as he realises he's not invited and wonders what he's going to tell the guys in the band.

Crossing the Border 1975

Gala wakes up on the couch next to the children. Her head is full of images from the night and she keeps reliving it. She chooses her clothes for work and feeds the girls some cereal at the table.

'You're going to stay with Tracy while Mummy goes to work today. I need to go make some money,' she says to Leah. 'Don't worry, I won't be long, you can play with Cindy, and if you're good, I'll bring you both some treats, okay?'

'Okay, Mummy, don't be tooooo long.'

Gala showers, pulls on her jeans and buttons up her blouse ready for work.

Tad is quiet and thoughtful as he drives her past the cornfields on the way to Ruby's.

'Thanks for the ride, Tad.' Gala is truly grateful and tries to start a conversation with this big brooding guy.

'Ain't no biggie, girl, have to git supplies anyways.'

'I'll be able to buy some food after my shift. Should make some tips.'

'Okay, that'll be good. Talk to Trace about food. She mostly gets TV dinners, doesn't really know how to cook. Mama did all that. You know how?'

'Yes, I learned to cook when I was a teenager,' Gala says proudly. 'Roast dinners and pasta are my specialty. Have you ever had a roast lamb dinner Tad?'

Tad cheers up, 'Roast lamb, eh? No can't say I have. Trace handles the food side; I mostly get beer and smokes.'

He drops her off at Ruby's. "Go get 'em tiger.'

Gala watches the long black Caddy cruise off down Main Street in the close muggy afternoon. She takes a deep breath and walks into the cool bar with a Lightning Hopkins track blasting and the swamp coolers working overtime. Elvis checks his watch as she walks up to the counter.

'On time, I like that!'

A lanky cowboy sprawled out at a table motions to Gala. 'Over here, Miss.'

She grabs a damp cork tray and goes to work.

'Git me two Buds and some Marlboroughs, honey. Here's forty bucks. You can keep the change. Make it quick though, I'm thirstier than an ol' camel in the desert.'

The shift goes quickly, and the boss let's her go when it gets quiet. Pushing open the bar door and returning to the outside world, Gala sees it's getting dark and the sky is streaked with purple and gold. She pats her right jeans pocket wondering how much she's made. Inside the phone booth she counts the sticky green bills. Ninety-eight dollars. She dials Tracy's number, but nobody picks up. Crossing the street to a Ma and Pa's General store she sees Johnny buying a six-pack of Tecates.

'Hi there, *mamacita*. How was your first day? You want a beer?'

'I'd love a drink. Actually, I need a ride home...'

Johnny puts his arm around her waist and draws her in close, 'Great, you drink. I'll drive. How did it go today? They didn't hassle you too much did they, Baby?'

'It was fine, thanks.' She's a little overwhelmed at this public affection. 'I have to get a few things.'

Johnny nods as she disappears down an aisle, grabbing cereal, eggs, bread, milk and some Sour Patch kids' candy she knows Leah likes.

The sleek Mustang is snaking down the dusty road as the night blanket sky folds in. Johnny seems quiet and thoughtful as Gala glances at him, picking up on his mood.

'I've been thinking I'd like to take you down home to meet my *familia*. We can take your kid. Leave tonight? He glances at Gala to see her reaction.

'Where's home?' She's surprised but pleased at his invitation.

'Guadalupe in Mexico, by the El Paso border. It's just a little place. My Mama and my sisters live there. I have to take them supplies and stuff.'

'It sounds like a long way. Is it?' She studies his profile.

'It's about a nine-hour drive, but you guys can sleep some of the way.' He turns and looks at her.

'I don't know,' she looks out the window. She hardly knows this gorgeous almost-too-good-to-be-true guy.

'C'mon, it'll be fun and it would be great having you ride shotgun. Gets lonely on that drive.'

His warm smile is infectious.

'Well, I suppose I could go, but what about your band?

'We're having a break this weekend. That's why it's a good time to go down there. We've been playing so damn much we could all use a break, from each other.' He chuckles. 'Besides the other guys have wives and kids they hardly ever see.'

'And I don't have to start work until next Saturday.'

'Yeah, same here *and* I really want my fam to meet you guys.'

Gala's sips on a cold Tecate. 'Okay then, but I don't speak Spanish *and* I have this funny Kiwi accent.'

Johnny laughs, 'That's okay, mija. Mama doesn't speak any English so y'all get along great. She loves kids too.'
Gala throws clothes into her battered leather suitcase and grabs Leah away from Sesame Street.

'Mummy's friend Johnny is taking us on a trip to Mexico. Say hello, darling.'

Leah smiles up at the tall giant and says 'hello' quietly.

'I'll be back in a few days, Tracy. Here's some cash, I made tips today.'

Trace looks up from a prostrate position on the couch and winks slyly. 'Y'all take care now. Thanks for the bread honey.' She swiftly stashes the bills into her grubby jean shorts.

Johnny is standing in the doorway watching Gala pack. 'Bring something to wear to church, girl. We'll go on Sunday.' He kisses the black onyx cross hanging on the silver chain around his neck.

Gala nods and folds her orange mini dress, squeezing it into the suitcase.

Little Cindy waves at Leah as they go out the trailer door.

❀

Johnny's Mustang is heading for the Mexican border. The widening Texas skyline stretches forever on either side of the long highway. Leah is asleep, cozied up on the back seat with a pillow and blanket. Gala's leaning back in the passenger seat with her eyes closed, listening to Johnny's blues collection.

'Wanta smoke, babe?' He passes Gala a joint, 'Not too strong this *mota*.'

Gala sleepily takes the offering, 'Just a little thanks.'

She inhales and watches the last of the purple-gold sunset, listening to B B King's *Do You Love Me?* She drifts into a dream.

Johnny's a Tex-Mex cowboy riding a tall black stallion through the Mojave Desert, his long hair flying out behind him, parting the dust clouds, coming to see her. She's waiting for him on the porch of an old Spanish villa, dressed in a long white lace dress. White roses are woven through her chestnut hair.

Gala opens her eyes and sees it's dark and misty outside. The clock on the dash says 4am.

'Sorry, I must've fallen asleep, Johnny. Must've been that joint. I was having a lovely dream though.'

Johnny chuckles. 'Yeah, you really crashed out, honey. Hope I was in your dream.' He smiles over at her. 'Hey, the good news is, we've travelled a good deal of the way while you were dreaming. We'll be at the border check soon. Don't worry, these agent dudes know me, I come down here so much.'

Gala studies his face, noticing he's exhausted from driving all night.

'Do you want me to drive? You could have a sleep?'

Johnny rubs his eyes and stretches, 'Nah, that's okay, babe. I'll just keep going. Let's get some coffee an' something to eat huh? There's a place I know in the next town, Sierra Bianca, just past these Apache mountains.'

Gala nods in agreement, relaxes in the comfortable leather seat and starts turning the radio dial.

'Mostly country and western stations down these parts and Mariachi music when you get closer to the border. You okay, baby?' Johnny checks her expression.

'Yes, I'm feeling happy to be on a road-trip with you. It's an adventure for me, like a movie. The scenery is so different from New Zealand. All these long stretches of never-ending highways and horizons. Just goes on forever. It's like we're in a technicolor western or something, hero and heroine on the run across the desert.' she laughs.

'Go on, tell me some more pretty words, *mamacita*.' He hams it up to make her laugh and dances in his seat to the mariachi song that's playing.

'That's nice music Johnny, wish I knew what it meant.'

'You'll pick it up, mija. I like this music too. My Papa was a great Mariachi player when he was alive, so handsome too, all styled out in his black n' white suit and big black Sombrero, yeah.' Gala watches him wipe his eyes. 'He got me started on the guitar, yeah taught me all the popular mariachi songs. Didn't like it when I started playing blues though. It was the Devil's music he used to say, black people's music.' Johnny gets quiet. Just the low rumbling of the motor and now Patsy Cline is falling to pieces on the radio. 'Border's a few miles ahead. Got your papers ready?' Johnny's tone is serious.

'Papers?' Gala is stunned.

'Just kidding, mija.' Johnny chuckles. 'These guys don't worry too much about you Anglos, just the brown faces.' He notices Gala's worried face.

'Don't worry, it'll be fine, baby. I'll get us through the *otra lado*, no problema.'

'I have my New Zealand passport and green card. No visa though. What about Leah?

Johnny puts his arm round her shoulders. 'It'll be cool. Good thing you got a green card though. How'd you get that?'

'Well, my husband is American, he's a musician too,' Gala says quietly.

'Husband huh, where is he at?' Johnny pulls the car over to the side of the road, the V8 rumbling as he rolls up a joint. He turns to study Gala's face, the passing car lights splash across his darkly handsome profile. 'He's not going to be after us, is he, honey?'

'No!' Gala is surprised at her own volume and quietens down. 'I've left him, run away actually. Yeah, we weren't getting along in LA. Fighting all the time.' She checks Johnny's reaction. 'I loved him and he's a really great musician. Played with some famous jazz players back in the day. He was always going on about how things would be better back in the States, but they weren't.'

'Oh, you met back in your country?'

'Yes, in a record store, actually. I loved our life in Auckland, but he was so homesick I guess, been gone from the States for years, never felt like he really belonged there. *Your fellow countrymen* he would say when he was angry about the government or something. We get to Los Angeles and the music scene had changed so much. He wasn't really connected like he used to be. He'd been away for fifteen years. So, he got a welding job to pay the rent. I was waitressing and trying to keep the home together. Billy got all depressed, started on the whiskey and complaining about the United States government, like he used to complain about the New Zealand one. It was a big wake-up call for me. I'd been following his dream, not mine. I always wanted to be a songwriter, performer you know.' She smiles shyly up at Johnny, having just revealed her life like an open book for him to take in.

'Well, it's a cool dream, babe.' He kisses her flushed cheek. 'And your voice is good too, sultry, sexy. Your old man was crazy to let you go.'

'Yeah,' Gala goes on thoughtfully, 'I left Billy while he was at work. Just grabbed my guitar, my kid and got on a bus to Texas. Just left a note and my wedding ring on the table. I feel really bad about that part.'

Herne Bay, Auckland, NZ, 1972, Summer, Sentinel Road Beach

Gala and Billy are chilling out on the beach with a tartan blanket and a picnic basket. Leah's playing in the foam of the waves, naked and giggling as the waves tickle her tiny feet. Billy's leaning on his side, smoking a Pall Mall, non-filter. Gala, in a cotton bikini, cuts up fruit for her daughter. Billy smiles as he watches his beautiful baby, playing in the water.

'Shit, it's a shame my mom can't see how cute her new granddaughter is. She'd love her. She loves babies. Well, what grandmother doesn't?'

'I know Billy. I'd love to meet your Mum too.'

'Now that Dave's gone to London, I've got nobody I relate to musically, you know? Maybe we could follow him? Stop off in California on the way and visit my family?'

'Sounds great! How much would that cost though?'

'A coupla grand maybe? I could ask my mom to help with some of it. I can't wait for you to see the States, babe. You'll love it there. The musicians are so hip, lots of great players. We could stay with my mom for a bit until we get jobs.'

'Aren't you happy here though, Billy? We have lots of friends and you're getting work. I have all my family here.'

'I'm just not challenged here. These Kiwi guys just don't groove. They're too uptight, you know? I can't go on doing these shitty cover band gigs much longer. I feel like a whore. You don't understand. Friends, schmends. I'm all about blowing, baby. Want to create some new original shit that will blow people away.'

Gala looks out to sea and watches the waves roll on to the little beach. She walks down and picks up Leah, wrapping her in a big colourful beach towel, cuddling her into her body. Billy lies back on the blanket, blowing smoke rings as the sun begins to set.

Crossing Over 1975

Johnny takes the next off-ramp and soon the Mustang pulls into to a car park right in front of Pam's All-Night Diner. A shapely black waitress looks up from the counter as Johnny and Gala come in through the screen door. Leah is flushed, sleeping in Johnny's arms.

Johnny smiles at the waitress, reads her nametag. 'Do you still do hotcakes, June?'

'For you, handsome, I can do the Special Grand Slam for $2.99. How many y'all want honey?'

'Two orders and two large coffees to go please, sugar, oh and some sugar.' He's tired but manages a friendly smile.

The waitress laughs as she sashays back to place their order. Johnny slaps twenty bucks down on the shiny counter and they go find a booth. Gala feels that all eyes are on them as they make their way down the aisle. Johnny lays the sleeping child down in the booth and they sit together on the other side. He puts his arm protectively around her. The cowboys show their obvious disapproval of interracial dating and shake their heads. Some scowl over at the tired travellers.

'Don't let these ignorant crackers spoil your meal, honey. They're not worth it. I've been dealing with this racist shit all my life. After a while you just learn to tune 'em out. They want us to react, so they can say, "look at that crazy Mexican going all psycho. Go back to your own country." *Pinche chingarros.*' He's getting fired up but manages to keep it under control.

June is laying down the worn but clean white napkins and silverware. She pours them water and looks over at Gala. 'Cute lil girl ya got there, honey. Y'all been travelling far?'

'All night actually, we've come from Denton tonight.'

'Y'all not from Texas though, are ya, honey?'

Gala feeling self-conscious as eyes are on her and she feels like everyone is listening. 'No, I'm from New Zealand.'

June comes back quickly, loaded with their food. Steaming hotcakes, smothered in maple syrup with melting butter drizzling down, stacked on thick white china plates and two large coffees. She manages to place it down all at once without spilling a drop and leaves with a warm smile. Gala is tired but impressed with such friendly service at that time of night.

'These are so light and scrumptious,' she says.

'I didn't know how hungry I was till I smelled them,' Johnny is shovelling down his pancakes and looks up as a young Mexican farmworker comes in and orders black coffee at the counter. He walks over to their booth.

'*Que pasa, hombre, como estas?*'

Johnny gets up and they 'brother' handshake.

'David, long time no visit.'

'Come over to the crib. There's a game on later.' David seems shy but friendly.

'Maybe later, homes, I have my *esposa* and her *bebe*. This is Gala.'

David smiles at her, 'No problema, Jesús's mom is home, *ese*. The boys'll love to see you.' David nods at Johnny and heads for the door.

Johnny finishes his pancakes, 'Time to roll, mija. Take this food with us huh?' He lifts up the limp-doll Leah, as Gala asks June for a doggy bag.

The Mustang is speeding down the 1-10. Grey light is breaking through the night sky. Big eighteen-wheelers are power-bully-driving down the long freeway. Johnny manoeuvres in and out of lanes. Diesel fumes and the heat from the road fill up the car.

'Hey, honey, ya wanta crash out for a while, grab a motel? Think I need some shuteye, or I'll go off the road. Highway hypnosis is kicking in.' He rubs his eyes.

'I could drive for a while Johnny.'

'On this freeway with all these speed-freak truckers?' Johnny punches the horn with anger as an enormous cherry red eighteen-wheeler pulls in front, nearly running them down.

'Nah, babe. I'd be too nervous. You've never driven my car before. It's got a powerful V8 engine. You gotta nurse it on these roads. Hey, look there's a place, Socorro Siesta Motel. Perfecto, we need rest and some help.' Johnny laughs out loud at his corny joke and takes the next exit.

He pulls into the parking lot of a rundown adobe motel, with red tile roofs and dirty-white-wooden shutters. The manager leads them down a cobblestone path to their room. It's clean and simple, whitewashed walls and a large wooden bed with a cross and rosary hanging on the wall above. There's a bible on the nightstand. Gala settles Leah in the cot and Johnny makes up their bed. Gala closes the shutters and the grainy early morning light reverts to night. Johnny takes off his cowboy boots and stretches out on the bed, his feet hanging over the edge.

'I'm gonna crash out, baby. Come and lie with me.'

Gala snuggles up to his warm body and feels him relax and

fall asleep. She watches his breathing, realizing she has fallen for him. Feels him in her core, warm, wanting, sensuous. Heavy trucks rumble past, shaking the ground. The town is waking up. She hears someone sweeping the pathway outside the window and sits up, quietly trying to pray, *Help us all arrive safely. Help us get through the border. Let me stay with Johnny forever.* Crying silently as she says the last part, she turns her damp face into his chest. Curled up next to him, she drifts off to sleep.

She dreams. She dreams that Johnny's still riding through the desert. A dark sombre storm is following him, lightning flashes. Behind in the dust, a group of dark riders emerge through the storm clouds in his pursuit...

Johnny is up, throwing open the shutters, letting in hazy sunlight, 'Better get on the road, babe. It's getting hot out there.'

'What time is it? I must have fallen asleep. Oh Leah, I see you found the yummy pancakes, eh?' Gala's voice is sleepy, and she laughs at the sight of her cherubic daughter covered in pancake crumbs and syrup. She's curiously looking around the room.

'Morning, Mummy, where are we?'

'We're going to Mexico darling, to see Johnny's family.'

'Yeay. Mummy, I need to pee.'

⸺⟞⟎◯⟎⟝⸺

Back on the road, Johnny puts on his sunglasses, shielding his eyes from the glare. 'Gotta go to the *mercado* now and get supplies for *mi familia.*'

'What's a *mercado*?'

'Geez girl you really don't know any Spanish do you. Market, *mercado*. It's right here. You guys stay in the car. I'll be right back.'

The *mercado* is teeming with people, all speaking loudly in Spanish. Bargaining with prices over vegetables, sacks of rice, beans and fruit. Little Taco stands line the sidewalk with simple cooking plates, stacks of corn tortillas and salsas. The smell of spicy chicken makes Gala hungry.

'Don't eat any of that crap. It'll make you sick.' Johnny pokes his head through the car window pointing at the stands.

He strides back to the car, laden with supplies, big sacks of rice, masa harina and pinto beans and throws them in the trunk. 'Those *chingarros* tried to charge me tourist prices. I chiselled them down though.' He laughs and winks at Gala. 'Hey, babe, you don't mind if we stop by my boys' place, do you? Play a quick game of cards. Show you two cuties off, say hallo?'

'Okay, sounds all right, I suppose.'

'Yeah, José and David they're always over at Jesús's place after work. We all came up together in Guadalupe.'

Johnny cruises the Mustang down the main street in El Paso. Late afternoon haze covers the honey mesquite trees as they pass through streets lined with modest wooden bungalows. He pulls into Jesús's driveway behind some Ford trucks and a red Camaro.

'This is his mom's place, his crib is in the back.' Johnny laughs. 'Yeah, he's got it all fixed up in the garage with a pool table and all sorts of gizmos. Television, pinball you name it.'

Leah follows him, skipping down the cobbled path. Gala holds her hand protectively.

'Will it be all right with Leah in there, with your boys?'

Johnny seems a little irritated, 'Jesús Gala, if it's a problem she can go over to his mom's house. Okay? You worry too much, mija.'

He pushes the door open into the garage. A cloud of skunky

weed smoke engulfs them. Tex-Mex blues is blasting out at full volume. Jesús greets them. His handsome-intense face lights up when he sees Johnny. The two friends hug in a strong brother-clinch.

'*Cómo estás hombre*, and who is this pretty *mamacita*?'

'This here's Gala and she comes all the way from Australia.'

'New Zealand actually.' Gala takes his warm outstretched hand and notices the strong veins from working in the fields.

'Nice to meet you, Jesús.'

'And who is this cute little *muchacha*?' Jesús beams down at her little girl.

'My name is Leah and I'm four.'

'She's a cutie, *ese*. Watch out for that little honey.'

José, his eyes sleepy from weed, has a scar on his left cheek. He steps out from behind the pool table, smiles at the girls then takes Gala's hand and kisses it in an old-worldly manner. He takes too long to let it go and winks cheekily at her.

Johnny gives him a dark warning-look.

'This *Mamacita* is mine, *ese, comprendes*?'

Jesús laughs, which eases the tension building in the room, and shows them into the den. The boys have been working on a bottle of tequila.

'José Cueve, the gold tequila, only the best for you, hombre.'

Jesús hands Johnny a full shot glass and slice of lemon. He tips a little salt on his palm, licks it, knocks back the gold liquid and bites into the lemon.

'*Tu quieres, mija*?' Jesús asks Gala. She shakes her head and accepts a cold Tecate beer from David, who's leaning up against an old fridge.

'Hey Johnny, we got some primo coca, your girl want some?' José winks at Gala, trying hard, she guesses, to impress her.

'No, she doesn't, *cabrón!*' Johnny glares at him.

Gala is feeling nervous around these hyped-up Latinos talking intensely in Spanish. José is lining up fat lines of coke on a mirror on the pool table, offering Johnny the first line. He snorts it quickly with a rolled up hundred-dollar bill.

'I'll take Leah to the house, to rest. Okay, Johnny?' Gala eyes him.

'Is your mom in, Jesús?' Johnny asks.

'Always, *cabrón*, always,' Jesús laughs.

Gala leads her daughter outside into the warm night, takes her delicate-gentle hand and they pass the frangipani flowers in terracotta pots along the cobblestone path. She drinks in the combination of sweet tropical scents mixed with fragrant pineapple sage. A frail Mexican *abuela* in a simple embroidered colourful dress answers the door.

'Hi, I'm Gala. I'm visiting with Johnny Magana. Would it be all right for my daughter to rest here for a while?'

Jesús's mother has the kindest brown eyes and the air of a tiny saint. 'Celia, *mucho gusto*,' she smiles warmly at Leah and shakes Gala's hand. 'No problema, honey. We have a spare room she can lie down there.'

Celia pads in her worn leather sandals down the polished wooden floor to the guest room, talking quietly to Gala. 'Those boys make too much noise for a little *muchacha*, and for you too, mija.'

'Thank you, *gracias*, Celia.'

Gala tucks Leah into the single bed covered in a colourful embroidered quilt and white linen cushions. She lights a candle under the picture of the Madonna and sits with her child until her pale eyelids grow heavy and she falls asleep. Gala finds Celia in the living room, stitching a fine lace square under the light of tall beeswax candles. A Mexican soap opera is quietly playing on the television set, covered with framed photos of the family.

Celia looks up when she approaches, '*Bebé* okay?'

'She's asleep now. Thank you. I'll be back soon, after Johnny finishes his card game.'

Celia looks straight into Gala's eyes. 'You never know how late that will be. *Cuidado, mija*, sometimes they get *loco* when they're altogether. Drink too much tequila.' She shakes her head, 'There's some bad blood between José and your Johnny from the old days, *cuidado*, okay? I'll watch the baby, don't worry.' Her expression is full of empathy.

'Thank you, Celia, *gracias*.' Gala heads back to the game room and hesitates outside the door, hearing the voices growing louder.

'C'mon, hombres, let's play! *Andalez, chingarros*!' She can hear that José is amped and ready to party.

Pushing the screen door open she sees Johnny seated at the card table with a full hand and another shot. He grins when he sees her, 'Hey, pretty baby, come and sit by me, bring me some luck. I'm gonna need it with these guys.'

The guys laugh. Fifty-dollar bills are piling up in the middle of the table and the José Quevo is drained.

'Hey Johnny man, you sure picked yourself up a cute little *gringa*, nice piece of ass, *cabrón*?' José is pretty out of it and leering at Gala.

'*Cuidado*, José, don't disrespect my girl now. What you got, Jesús, you playing or what?'

Jesús is doing another fat line.

'What *you* got Johnny, besides your sexy *gringa*?' says José menacingly.

Johnny's dealing another hand, beads of sweat on his forehead. He gives José a dark look.

'Watch what you say, *cabrón*! I'm getting sick of your shit, man! You say one more thing about Gala and you're going down.'

José laughs dangerously, enjoying Johnny's reaction. 'Okay, man, okay! It's the coca, makes you say crazy-loco-shit.'

Johnny relaxes and puts his arm around Gala, kisses her on the cheek and the poker resumes.

'Want a line, pretty Gala?' José is not giving up.

Gala refuses the staggering line of coke with schoolgirl politeness. 'No thanks, José.'

José snorts up the whole gagger and comes up for air, shaking his head. 'Whoa, *chinga del madre*. This is some pure shit, hombres!'

The boys laugh. José turns his hyped-up attention to Gala, 'C'mon, mija, sure you don't want to try some? It'll get you sooo horny.'

Johnny jumps to his feet, knocking the card table over. He grabs José by his shirtfront. 'I'm so sick of your pinche-jealous-shit, man! Jealous of everything I got. Now you want my girl too? In front of me? That's over the line, *cabrón*!'

Johnny's solid punch sends José over on the pool table. José gets to his feet with a pool cue in his right hand. Johnny grabs the other cue. They circle the pool table like wild dogs, eyes fixed on each other. Like slow motion, the music fades to white noise. José's skull cracks as Johnny swings around, whacking him on the side of the head. José falls on the ground with an ominous thud. Jesús and David go to help him up and see he's bleeding out all over the floor.

The Getaway, July 1975

Johnny's still wired, talking fast, his eyes fixed ahead. 'God what have I done, mija? We can't let my *familia* know about what went down with José, Okay? Yeah, don't mention anything about that, no way!' He is full of remorse, overcome. 'Mama doesn't need anymore bad news. She thinks I'm doing so well with my band, you know, don't want to spoil the illusion. My mama doesn't speak any English, *no habla inglés*, yeah my sisters speak some. My brother Javier and I are the only ones who got out of that town. There was no future for us there. Everyone's so poor, struggling, barely surviving, *comprendes?*'

Gala listens to him, not saying much. The vision of the fight still strong in her mind, the thud of José's head, the blood.

'Mama's not been the same since Pop died. They really loved each other. She's lost without him, they were such a team. She keeps herself busy. Yeah, Pop worshipped her. His first love and hers. They got married in springtime at the little chapel in Guadalupe and never ever moved from that town. Can you imagine?'

'That's so romantic though, Johnny, sweet.'

Johnny's definitely on a roll. 'Javier and I left here in our teens. Couldn't find work in that town after high school. We wanted to see the rest of the country. Javier had some bad luck with Johnny Law, now he's inside *Chino* for armed robbery. He's still got ten years left to serve, such a waste. Mama can't talk about him. He was the baby. She spoiled him. Being the oldest, I took on the responsible role in *mi familia*. They all count on me now that Pop's gone and Javier's inside.'

'When my parents broke up, I had to do that too,' Gala says quietly, 'I cooked the meals every night when my mother had to go to work. I was fifteen and it was hard with schoolwork and exams, but I had to look after my younger sisters a lot. Mum was often depressed after the divorce. I'm pretty used to surviving.' She looks up at him, but his eyes were on the road.

'God, what have I done, mija?

There is no sign of people for miles. The Rio Grande runs like a bright glistening teal-ribbon next to the highway. Johnny takes the exit to Guadalupe. Gala notices that life is more impoverished on this side of the border. The road to Guadalupe is dusty and loaded with potholes, which Johnny dodges with skill. It's a bumpy ride. He gets excited when a white walled chapel comes into view.

'There's my town.' It's like driving back in time. Rusty farm-trucks parked on cobblestone streets, horses tied up outside the general store. 'Yahoo, we'll be in time for *pan dulce,*' Johnny is happy-upbeat.

'What's that, something to eat?' Gala is trying to keep up. She's hungry and tired from the road.

'Oooooh, girl, wait till you taste them. My sisters make them to sell in town. They make the best *pan dulce* around here. Sweet cakes, you know. They always save the sweetest for home. Sweet like you, *mi preciosa.'*

Johnny swings the Mustang into a park outside a small adobe house, set back from the road. Brightly coloured poppies, marigolds and passionflowers line the fenced garden.

'Remember, baby, not a word.' His eyes are still dilated from the coke. He kisses Gala fully on the mouth, then jumps out of the car and strides towards the house. Voices chatter excitedly in Spanish inside. A pretty grey-haired Mexican woman in a

black dress and red apron splattered with flour, rushes out
to greet him and they hug tightly. Her hair is braided with
colourful ribbons, tears run down her lined face, and she
doesn't let him go.

'Gala this is my beautiful Mama, Gabriela. This is Gala,
Mama, *mi novia*.'

She smiles as she greets Gala and kisses her on the cheek.

Taking Leah by the hand Gabriela, leads them into the house.

'Not a word, our secret, mija,' Johnny whispers in Gala's ear.

Inside Gabriela's kitchen, white-washed-adobe walls and thick dark wooden bench tops, two tall sisters, sort pastries into woven reed baskets. The wood oven throws warm light into the kitchen, with large cast-iron pots bubbling on the stove. Bright red chilies dry in bunches from the ceiling.

The girls look up as Johnny walks in with his arm around Gala.

'Gala, these are *mis hermanas*, Helena and Primavera,' Johnny is proud of his *familia* and happy to be back home. He beams.

'Hola,' Gala is shy. The sisters are beautiful, long dark hair and almond-shaped kind brown eyes. One has freckles, the other doesn't, she notes.

'Hi, Gala. Nice to meet you, *mucho gusto*,' Primavera and Helena offer their hands, smiling with the same charm as their brother.

They all shake hands rather formerly. Standing on the terracotta tiled floor, feeling the soft palms of the girls and taking in all the colours and cooking aromas of this charming kitchen, Gala feels at home too. Even though she doesn't understand what the women are saying most of the time, she can tell by their tone and laughter that they have fun together and a deep love for each other. It reminds her of her own sisters.

'*Queires chocolate, muchachas?*' Do you want hot chocolate?' Johnny asks.

Gala and Leah nod. She's still holding Gabriela's hand and the sisters are kneeling down, making a fuss of her.

'*Que linda*, look at her hair, *que rubio.*' The girls fluff Leah's hair, making her giggle.

Gabriela wipes her hands on her apron and begins to grind the sugary chocolate block with a wooden stirrer. The rich dark chocolate froths up as she twirls it around the ceramic bowl. Leah is sitting on the bench top, watching.

'*Molinillo, muy authentico,*' Gabriela tells her smiling.

Soon they are all sitting around the long dark mesquite table, sipping the sweet chocolate in thick white cups. Johnny chats easily with his Mama in Spanish. Gala watches his expressions, seeing he's radiant, overjoyed to be there. He turns to translate for Gala. 'Mama says we came at a good time. There's a big celebration this weekend, a religious holiday, a special occasion for Guadalupe. Mama is pretty religious, like me,' he chuckles, 'after that we'll have to go, okay?'

'That's a shame Johnny, I was beginning to feel at home here.'

Johnny's eyes are intense, and he whispers, 'Baby, we have to go back, don't make it harder for me.'

'Sorry Johnny, I'm trying to forget all about what happened. It all seems like a horrible dream.'

He hugs her into him and she smells his warm skin, feels his arms around her, safe. Johnny's sisters are listening, watching their brother and Gala as they work. They talk quietly together. Primavera hands Leah a steaming sugar-coated pan dulce, which the little girl immediately dunks in her hot chocolate. The sisters and Gabriela laugh at Leah's ecstatic expression, as she tastes the sweet, warm pastry for the first time. The atmosphere is amiable and harmonious. Some bantams begin scratching round the kitchen door. Helena shoos them away with a straw broom. Leah squeals when she sees the pretty speckled hens and helps Helena shoo them outside. Gala leans against the faded brick-red doorway, gazing at the outdoor scene. A bony white goat chews dry grass in the backyard. Two faded sports Mustangs sit, rusting in the harsh sun. The long clothesline flaps with bleached white sheets and tablecloths. Cotton puffy clouds hang in the cerulean sky.

'Shame about Javier's cars, huh?' Johnny passes her, bringing in more groceries. He adopts a Texan accent, 'That's all the supplies, Maaam.'

Everyone laughs as he drops the sacks down on the floor.

He joins Gala at the backdoor, 'We're cooking up a big feast tonight. They're really happy with all the food I bought at the *mercado*. We'll have enchiladas, frijoles, chili rellenos and Mama's famous handmade tortillas. You like Mexican food, right?'

'What I've tried has been all right, Del Taco or Taco Bell?'

'Oh, nah, baby, that crap isn't real Mexican food. That's gringo style. Wait till you taste the real thing. You'll never go back. *Authentica mija.*'

'Great, can't wait, I'm getting hungry. Johnny, where can we get washed up?' She's looking at Leah's beaming face, covered in chocolate and pan dulce crumbs.

Jonny picks up Leah in his arms. 'Come this way, you're in for a rustic treat, *chicas.*'

He leads them outside to the washhouse. A huge copper tub stands on the earthen floor. He starts hand-pumping water into it. Leah chases the bantams out when they come in, laughing as they run around her, clucking and flapping. Johnny lights the kindling under the copper.

'Should be warm soon girls. I better go help Mama with the meat, have to make the marinade.' He kisses Gala on the cheek, and she watches him stride happily back to the house, singing to himself. The water starts sending bubbles up from below and she stirs it around with her hand. Leah peeks over the top watching the swirling patterns, feeling the steam on her face.

'What would it be like to live down here, Leah? No television, no electric oven. A wood stove and copper tub for our bath. I'd have to learn how to make tortillas by hand, I suppose. It's quite lovely here, don't you think? Simple and slowed down,' she's talking to Leah but more to herself.

Primavera enters the washhouse, holding a pile of white

sun-bleached towels and creamy vanilla soap. She smiles at Gala. 'Here, Johnny said give you for bath?'

'Thanks so much, *gracias*,' Gala takes the towels from her slender outstretched arms.

'Johnny, okay? No in trouble, he okay? Looks wild in the eyes, like an animal, *loco*. He been partying?' Primavera talks quietly.

'No, don't worry, everything's okay,' Gala lies quietly. 'Johnny's just tired. He's been driving for hours. He's excited to be with you all. Thanks for the towels.'

Primavera turns to go and sees Leah, naked, chasing the chickens out. She grabs a whiskbroom and helps her. The chickens fuss and cluck their way out. Then she laughs and goes back to the kitchen.

Gala lowers Leah into the warm tub then undresses and joins her. She lies back in the warm water, watching Leah try to wash her own hair with the bar of soap. Leah's hair is full of bubbles.

'I like it at Johnny's house, Mummy. Can we stay here, please? Ooh look my friends are back.'

She clambers out of the tub, hair frothy with soap, grabs a towel and tries to flap the chickens out. Wrapping herself in the big white towel she peaks outside to see if they're out there. Gala chuckles at her daughter's comical antics as she washes her own skin with the creamy soap, washing away her tiredness and fear.

Johnny shows them back inside the house. Feeling clean and refreshed Gala follows his lead, her bare feet pattering down the tiled hallway to a small, whitewashed room. Leah skips between them, chattering to Johnny about the chickies. There are two single beds with bleached white sheets and pillows and a woven

Mexican blanket rolled at the end. A wooden cross hangs over a modest well-worn wooden desk with a framed photo of a tall handsome mariachi player smiling and playing an oversized Spanish guitar. The only other item in this modest room is a dark wooden guitar leaning against the closet door. Johnny drops Gala's suitcase on the bed and picks up the photo.

'Yep, that's the man who got me started on guitar, Jesús Magana. What a legend! Where are you now, Pops, playing for the *angelitos*?'

'The chickies came in the wash house, Johnny,' Leah tells him.

'You like those little chickies huh? *Pollitos*, puk, puk, puk.' Johnny does a chicken dance as he goes out the door, flapping his folded arms and wiggling his behind. 'Puk, puk, puk.'

Leah tries to copy him, and they all laugh. Johnny leaves the girls to dress. Gala tries on a white lacy dress she'd brought with her and checks the effect in the mirror. Leah is attempting to pull her dress on and gets it on backwards and inside out. Gala sorts her daughter's red dress out, brushes her angelic curls and buttons her up. They both slip on their leather sandals and follow the delicious smells coming from the kitchen.

Inside Gabriela's *cocina* there is much activity going on. Huge cast iron pots bubbling with beans, Gabriela is rolling tortillas on the wooden bench-top while the sisters chop onions and tomatoes for salsa.

'Can I help?' Gala asks Helena.

'Guacamole, you know how? Just mash avocadoes, okay? And garlic, ooh and a *poco limon*?'

Helena sets Gala up at the bench with a ceramic bowl, avocadoes, lemons, garlic, knife and masher. Gala starts to work and Gabriela stops rolling to tie a tea towel around her waist.

'*Vestida es muy bonita, Gala. Buena mija, gracias, buena.*' She smiles at Gala and feels the lace in the dress between her worn fingers.

'You dress is so pretty,' Helena translates for Gala.

'*Gracias,*' Gala thanks her.

Johnny puts a six-pack of Tecates in the icebox, a big cupboard in the adobe wall with a huge block of ice inside. He pops open a cold beer, sits down at the table with the Spanish guitar and tunes it up. Leah clambers up beside him on the table, curious.

'This was my Pop's favourite guitar. He had it made especially in Guadalajara. Check out the rosewood, mija, and mother of pearl inlay.'

Gala smiles over at him. 'Play us a song please Johnny?'

Gabriella and his sisters nod in agreement, not missing a beat with their food prep.

'Okay, this one's for you, Mama,' he fingerpicks a melodic Latin tune. Gabriela nods and smiles as she continues to roll perfectly round tortillas.

'*Y por eso los grandes amores de muchos colores me gustan a mi.*' Johnny sings from his heart. 'This song's all about the colours of the country and how we love them. It was Pop's most requested song. The United Farmworkers sing it at their meetings. Yeah, Pop supported Cesar Chavez and his movement. He had plenty of friends who went to America for a better life and ended up working the rest of their lives in really hard conditions, for very little money. If they complained or ever asked for a raise, the farmers would threaten them with deportation. Cesar is working on changing all that. Yeah, he goes right out into the fields on a tractor and tells the farmworkers that they have rights. They're employed by the American farmers, so they have rights, illegal or not. That guy's a legend, *ese*,' Johnny is obviously passionate about this subject.

He continues to fingerpick the song and Leah sits, spell bound, while his large fingers rhythmically pluck the nylon strings. The kitchen is filling up with delicious savoury aromas. The sisters are lightly frying the tortillas and stacking them in a wicker basket, their big bowl of salsa glistens on the table.

Johnny stops playing, 'Hey, baby, why don't you play one of your songs?' he asks Gala and then to his mother, 'She has the voice of an angel, Mama.'

'Can you play for real?' Primavera looks up from the fry pan, interested.

'Just a bit,' Gala is embarrassed by all the attention. 'Not like Johnny. I'm just a beginner really.' She washes the avocado mush from her hands, takes the guitar from Johnny.

She strums the handsome instrument, feeling all the years of playing and soul bound in the rosewood body. She starts to sing.

Man and I were fighting, almost everyday
So I took out all of my savings, had to get away
Took the things I couldn't leave behind
Daughter and guitar
Knew a friend in Denton, Texas
Didn't think it was far...

Gala is overcome with emotion and stops playing. Johnny puts his arm around her and kisses her gently on the cheek, shiny with her tears.

'You sing very pretty, Gala, but what happens at the end?' Primavera asks.

Gala slowly gets her nerve back and continues.

Bus station in LA, where I bought my ride
Said they figured they'd get into Denton
Round about midnight
Daughter lay there sleeping
Phoenix moon hung low
Just me and my dreaming
So much I didn't know
Thinking how my man would feel
Coming home after work
Finds the note I had written
Tears streaming the dirt
I didn't mean to hurt him so
All I knew was I had to go

The women all stop working and listen, eyes glistening.

'That song is so sad, Gala, that a real story, huh?' Primavera is the first to speak.

'Well yes, I suppose it is and you're right it is kinda sad.'

Leah starts to clap, 'Yeah for Mummy, yeah for Johnny.'

Everyone laughs. Gala goes back to her guacamole and Johnny fingerpicks some impressive blues licks. Gala enjoys being part of this family, scooping the avocadoes out of their shells and mashing them to a smooth pulp. Her own family is thousands of miles away and she misses them like crazy at times. But she is still haunted by the pool cue swinging, the sound of it hitting José's skull, Johnny's face. She can't stop the images flashing in her mind.

Dinner proceeds with much enjoyment and laughter. The enchiladas are amazing. Gala's never tasted anything so tasty, but she doesn't eat them all. Johnny is drinking Tecates, relaxing and not eating much either. Gala can tell he's tired. His eyes look sleepy.

'You want to rest for a while Johnny?'

'Just for a little while, baby, then we'll have to get back on the road. Sorry mama.' He puts his arm around the little woman. '*Trabajo, mucho dinero, Mama.*' He peels some hundred-dollar bills from his money roll and hands them to her.

Gala helps her drunken Romeo down the hallway. He's heavy and weaving but she manages to help him fall on to the bed, takes off his boots and wipes his sweating forehead with a damp facecloth. She sits down beside him on the narrow bed. Johnny's head is propped up against the starched white pillows, his eyes are sleepy and his long black hair spills out. He wants to get this off his chest, this weight that's pressing on them like a sinister shadow, creeping into all corners of their lives.

'I messed up José pretty bad, mija. I can't drink spirits, always fucks me up, or do coke for that matter. Bad combination.' He shakes his head, ashamed. 'José used to be my best friend down here. We had a good band in High School. Yeah, he played bass, real good, bitchin' actually. Now he's mad and jealous at how my life turned out in Texas. He's still working on a ranch down here, hates it. I just saw red when he kept disrespecting you, baby. He got me so fucking angry, I lost it. God, I wish we'd never gone to that *pinche* game.'

Gala listens as he tells his truth, wiping sweat from his forehead.

Johnny pulls her to him and they lie together. 'I want to make love with you, so crazy about you, mija.'

'Johnny it's your Mum's place, I don't feel right about it.' Gala whispers.

Johnny tries to change her mind with his warm kisses. He undoes the buttons down the back of her lace dress. Gala slowly takes off his shirt and lies next to his warm, tight body. They kiss, long searching kisses, then she feels Johnny shaking and realises he is sobbing. They lie with arms around each other. Gala feels him relax and breathe deeply into sleep. She wiggles out of his arms, puts on her white dress and pads down the tiled hallway to the bedroom where Leah is sleeping.

⚬—⊕◯⊕—⚬

Early morning light is streaming in through the shutters.

Johnny is standing over Gala, hyped up and anxious. 'C'mon Gala. We gotta get outta here, now! Those guys'll be round here, wanting revenge. As long as I'm not here, they won't hurt my *familia*. C'mon, get your kid, baby, let's *vamanos*!'

Gala walks quickly down the hall with a sleepy Leah in tow. Gabriela is already up. She's in the living room, kneeling and praying in front of a candle. She's whispering a prayer, kissing the black onyx cross from around her neck.

angel de mi guarda
dulce compania
ne me desampares
ni de noche de dia

Gardian angel
Sweet companion
Don't abandon me day or night

She turns and smiles with tearful eyes at Gala and her child, standing framed in the arched doorway.

'Bye, Gabriela, *gracias*,' Gala blows her a kiss.

Back on Interstate 10, 1975

The black Mustang is speeding down Interstate 10, heading back to Denton. Johnny lights up a joint and offers it to Gala, but she doesn't partake, choosing to be clear-headed. She's worrying about what is coming next on this road trip and just what she has gotten herself into. Leah feels her mother's tension and clambers over to cuddle on her lap like a puppy.

Johnny is quiet, beads of sweat on his brow, thoughtful.

'I'm so sorry, mija. I'll make it up to you guys, I promise. We'll go do something fun when we get home okay? I feel so bad about everything. I should never have hooked up with those *pinche* lowlifes. They're always trouble. That's why I left my town.'

Gala doesn't know how to reassure him. She reaches out and puts her warm hand on his, squeezing gently, forcing a smile.

'I could teach you some more guitar, Gala, you really have the voice of an angel. You could make a living at it, write songs, do shows, y'know. I'd like to teach you some new blues patterns and things like that.'

Gala is charmed by his enthusiasm. 'I'd love that Johnny. I've never been taken that seriously, but sure, I would love to do all that stuff more than anything in the world.'

Johnny is smiling, eyes shining. 'You really can if you want, if you believe in yourself, honey. You guys staying at my place tonight? I was really beat last night. Let me make it up to you, huh?'

'I'd like that Johnny. What about Leah, somewhere for her to sleep?' Gala is pleased despite her sensible voice.

'No sweat, I have a comfortable couch for lil' missy.'

'I'd love to spend the night with you, Johnny,' she says shyly, looking up at his strong profile.

'Here's *mi casa* girls.'

Johnny pulls into the overgrown driveway of a modest whitewashed cottage. Vines and lilac flowers fall from the roof and the windows have green shutters. A Siamese cat curls around Johnny's legs as he unlocks the front door.

'Girls, meet Freddy my *gato*. He's friendly and very hungry, *pobrecito*.'

'Here Freddy, Freddy.' Leah kneels down to stroke the sleek feline who is curling around her short legs, purring loudly.

'Oh, he likes you already, mija.'

Johnny fills a bowl with dry cat food and scratches Freddy's ears as he devours the biscuits ravenously. A huge black and white poster of Jimi Hendrix in a military jacket hangs above a patchwork-covered couch.

'Here Leah, you'll be comfortable with a blanket, won't you? Freddy might sleep with you if you're nice to him. Now what would my girls like for dinner?'

'Hamburglars, hamburglars and chips please,' Leah looks up at Johnny with a cheeky grin.

'Then hamburglars it is. Let's go, *vamonos*!'

The hungry trio are soon strolling back to Johnny's from Whataburger, loaded with giant burgers and big piping hot fries. Leah is blowing on a French fry as she skips along next to her mum. The Denton streets are filled with small white wooden houses. Sweet, scented jasmine spills over their picket fences. Johnny is whistling.

'Just like the all-American family, huh girls?'

'Big chips eh, Mummy? I mean fries.' Leah is munching one and skipping ahead of them.

'I wish it could be like this, Gala. Simple family life, no hassles you know, you and me doing family stuff, right?' Johnny smiles at her.

Gala nods but knows he's only dreaming, and that danger is only hours from destroying everything. She's numb inside, scared for all of them. After they've devoured the best burgers in Texas, Johnny gets up from the table.

'I'm beat, baby, gonna crash out for a while. There's sheets and a pillow for her in the hall closet. Night, Leah.'

'Nitey nite, Johnny.'

'See you in the *mañana, chica.*'

Johnny takes off his boots and heads for his room off the hall.

'Will you stay with me, Mummy?' Leah has a pleading look in her eyes.

'Yes darling, I'll stay with you until you fall asleep, my little munchkin.' Gala sponges her sleepy daughter's face and tucks her in with a sheet on the couch. She sings a quiet lullaby as she watches Leah's eyelids lower. It's a lullaby her mother always sang to her. 'Too ra loo ra loo ra, hush now don't you cry.'

The simple cottage is quiet. Gala picks up a beautiful acoustic Gibson, leaning in the corner and takes it out to the screened-in-porch. Crickets are a constant hum in the background. She picks out her new song on the nylon strings, remembering her dream of Johnny in the desert, with the dark clouds behind.

I saw your smile was sweet and your heart was true and you were my man

I looked inside your gypsy eyes and knew that you were my man.

Gala enters Johnny's room quietly. Blue-silver moonlight streams through the shutters. She's wrapped her hair up in a big black towel after her hot shower. It feels heavenly to be clean, smelling of vanilla. A candle flickers on the side table next to a small statue of the Guadalupe virgin. Johnny's sleeping soundly, lying stretched out across the bed in white boxers. She cuddles up to him, lightly runs her palm over his warm, brown muscular arms and kisses him on his neck and shoulders. Johnny wakes up slowly and caresses her back, down between her legs, whispering sweet sexy things in her ear. He's on top of her and they're making love, like in a dream.

They lie quietly after. Gala is sweaty – blissed out – feeling the effects of their intense, heartfelt lovemaking. Johnny reaches up and switches on the swamp cooler, blowing cool damp air on their naked bodies.

'Feel like a smoke, babe?' Johnny asks her.

'What time is it? Sure, why not. You want a coffee, babe?'

'Sure, why not? You know where the coffee is?'

Johnny is rolling a joint when Gala re-enters the room with two steaming cups of Mexican coffee.

'*Gracias, mija*, you're as sweet inside as you are outside. I could fall in love with you, you know that?'

'Thanks Johnny. I think you're pretty sweet too, in a dangerous kinda way.'

'Dangerous, huh? You like bad boys, do you? He pulls her to him and kisses her deeply. They fall back to sleep in each other's arms.

Hours later she wakes up and Johnny has gone. She sees

on the little bedside clock that it's 6 a.m. and she finds him making breakfast. Leah's perched up on a bar stool, putting cherry tomatoes in a wooden bowl, chatting away to the chef. Gala smells the delicious crisp bacon frying and coffee brewing in his cheery sunny kitchen. She's pulled on one of his clean denim shirts and kisses him on the cheek as he flips the eggs.

'Fresh coffee in the pot, babe. We gotta leave right after breakfast. Need to get your bags together, pronto.'

'Thanks, yeah no worries.'

'Morning, darling,' she says to Leah. 'You're a good girl helping Johnny.'

He is serving up the steaming eggs, bacon and hash browns, 'Can you turn the news on, baby? Channel Nine, Dallas station.' His tone is anxious.

She clicks on the Channel Nine news. It's the end of a Budweiser commercial. *This just in, blues guitarist wanted for murder in Texas border town. Twenty-six-year-old farm-worker, José' Valdez, killed after brawl in El Paso. Johnny Magana, guitarist for the popular blues band, The Dallas Rhythm Aces, named as the suspect. Texas Police are on the trail for the suspect believed to be travelling in a black Mustang with a young, foreign woman and small child.*

Gala is sick with fear, realizing she is involved in the crime. Johnny stands, frozen, blood draining from his face.

Leah looks up from her breakfast, 'Look, Mummy, Johnny's on the News.'

Johnny's handsome mug is full screen in a press shot with the band.

'Holy shit, holy Mother of God, I killed José! Help me God.' He's completely shaken, tears falling.

Gala goes to comfort him, but he pushes her away.

'Don't touch me, Gala! I'm a killer. I've killed someone. You've got to hate me. How will Mama ever forgive me?' Johnny drops down on the couch and stares blankly at the screen, mesmerized.

'Johnny what are you going to do? You'll have to turn yourself in. It'll be manslaughter, you didn't mean to *kill* him. We'll have to get a lawyer!' Gala kneels down in front of him, trying to reach him.

Johnny doesn't reply, but gets up and goes into his room and starts throwing clothes into a rucksack. Gala watches him from his doorway, feeling fear and adrenalin pumping.

'Well, if you're coming with me, you better get your stuff together and get your kid into the car!' His tone is sharp and shoots through Gala. He's never spoken to her like that before. She's afraid of what he may do next, feeling powerless to stop him.

Johnny peels out of his driveway, dust flying and is gunning the Mustang hard, back on to the freeway. His face is pale with beads of sweat on his brow, wide eyes focused on the road ahead.

'Think I'm going to jail? No way in hell, baby! Ya think they're going to care about another crazy Mexican in Texas? They expect us to act crazy-loco. No Texas judge is ever gonna give me a light sentence, little Miss White-Bread-Anglo! Manslaughter, yeah right! Don't you know how it works here in the great USA? There're rules for the 'Good Ol' Boys' to break and get away with and then there's rules for us minorities!' His voice is getting louder and his knuckles are white, gripping the steering wheel. 'Yeah, black brothers have it worse than my brown brothers. At least they don't usually hang us up to rot. No, mija, they deport us and shove us in jail to rot. You should see how many of us are inside. Mexican Mafia is huge in there. If you don't play by their rules, *adios*, you're dead, baby. Ya' think I want to get gang raped by some White Power motherfuckers?'

Gala puts her hands over Leah's ears. She's crawled on to her mother's lap, frightened by the shouting.

'You're scaring her Johnny.'

'I'm sorry, babe,' he drops his volume but not the intensity, 'but I would rather kill myself than go inside. I have to get outta town. Get down to Mexico, way south. That's all I can do. I'm truly sorry, mija. I can't have you part of this mess. You and Leah, no, it's too dangerous.' He's whispering hoarsely. 'Just tell the cops you don't know where I went and you don't know anything about the fight. You were in the house with the *abuela*, okay? Will you do that for me? I could send for you guys when I get down there, if you still want me?'

'I'll stay with you. We can make it out of here. I love you, Johnny Magana.'

'I love you, Gala.' He leans over and kisses her sweetly, tears beginning to roll down his beautiful face.

Gala wishes right now that he wasn't so handsome. It's like she is under his spell and it's powerful, intoxicating, like a drug which she can't pull away from. She's thinking about their getaway options, heart pounding.

'Johnny, baby, listen. Let's stop at the trailer. Maybe Tad can help us with a ride to the border or maybe you guys could swap cars or something? That would throw the cops off the track, right?'

'I still don't know about you and the kid though, mija.' He's frowning, eyes on the road.

'Hey, you could change your appearance, you know, maybe cut your hair? Tad said he was going to sell the Caddy anyway. See, two heads are better than one?' She's trying to sound upbeat-stand-by-my-man but inside she's sick with fear.

'Look, girl, you don't understand. This isn't the movies, okay? My boys are dangerous, and they'll be after my blood now, revenge for José. And let's not forget about the police?' He's quiet for a beat then says, 'Okay, what the hell, come along, but I can't promise you a safe ride with those assholes after us. *Sangre,* that's what they're after, my blood.'

The Mustang pulls into the trailer park and Gala and Leah go inside Tad and Tracy's trailer.

Tracy's up, smoking, drinking coffee and looking hung over.

'Y'all with your guitar man?'

'Yeah,' Gala looks down at the shag carpet which looks even more off-white.

'Well honey, your Johnny man is all over the news, y'all should check it out. They said he killed some Mexican guy? Hey Tad, y'all watching them eggs?'

Tad strides in with a Bud in one hand and a soggy stogy in the other. He quaffs the beer and smirks at Gala. 'Sure picked a winner there, girl. You an' the kid want some eggs?'

'Thanks Tad.'

Johnny enters and fills the doorway. Tracy comes alive.

'Oh hi, Johnny Babe. You've just been on TV, hot stuff.'

Cindy runs in and grabs Leah's hand. They run to the bedroom and both start jumping on the saggy bed with gusto. Gala attempts to eat the overcooked eggs but isn't hungry.

'Coffee?' Tad asks her. He pours her some and they all sit around the table. Johnny breaks the silence.

'Tad, think you could you help us out? Could you trade your

Caddy for my Mustang?'

'Throw in some Franklins and y'all might have yourself a deal.' Tad smirks again.

Tracy exhales on her menthol and looks right at Gala.

'Ya know we don't want no trouble around here, honey. Tad and me could get thrown out,' her tone is harsh.

'I know. Trust me. We want to get out of Denton fast.' Gala means it.

Tracy's eyes narrow. 'Soon as possible. Cops'll be round here asking questions. I mean you went down to Mexico together, right? That makes you a necessity or somethin', right Tad?'

'Accessory, dumbass,' Tad rolls his eyes at his sister. 'I suppose I could paint that Mustang and change the plates? Sell it on, maybe?'

'Man. I really appreciate it.' Johnny hands Tad a fat roll of hundred-dollar bills. They brother handshake.

'I think y'all better get moving. I'll stash your car someplace till this all blows over. Don't want no pigs pokin 'round here, man.' Tad eyeballs Johnny as they exchange car keys.

Johnny goes to start the engine.

Tad pulls Gala aside. 'You better get right away from here, girl. Go back home to Australia, don't look back, that's my advice. You git away from that crazy Mexican. He's in all kinda shit now, on the run. Cops'll be all over his brown ass. You hear me?' Tad is dead serious.

'Thanks for everything Tad,' Gala kisses him on his prickly cheek.

Tad comes back from outside and hands Johnny some 8-tracks from the Mustang. 'Here, *hombré*, you want these? There's only a cassette player in the Caddy, yeah, it even records, came with the car. Hey there's another way back to the freeway. Go by the swamp down behind the park, on that dirt road. It hooks up by the railroad. Go down south a-ways and you'll see the 10. Take care, man.'

The yellow cornfields stream past like paint rippling. Johnny's hauling ass down the country road, fish tailing round bends. Gala is praying they all stay alive, cuddling Leah, looking up at him, her eyes pleading. The smooth Freeway 10 is soon under their tires and Johnny adopts a more responsible speed.

'We'll make some miles, then let's stop at a motel by the border. Can you help me shave off my hair, mija?'

Gala looks at his shiny long back tresses, running her hand over his head. 'My Sampson is losing his beautiful black hair.'

'Yeah, I'll definitely look different like that. Get new IDs there, that'll give us some time too. Who do you want to be? We gotta get our plan together. Hey, grab those maps in the door pocket would you, babe. I gotta check the route.' Johnny's driving intensely with his mind in escape mode.

'Looks like there's a crossover at Laredo,' Gala notices.

'Yeah, that's good, then south towards the beaches. I've got cash, we'll be all right for a while. After that we'll have to sing for our supper.' He winks at Gala and laughs out loud, but his laugh has no joy. Its hollowness fills up the car.

'No sign of the boys yet, or the cops.' Johnny's keeping an eye on the rear-view mirror, switching lanes on the wide freeway heading south to San Antonio.

✦

The Cadillac slides into a park outside a cheap motel. The people in the streets are all Mexican. Gala feels conspicuous with her sandy hair and blondie-gringa-child as she carries her bags inside. The room is clean, bare, with one double bed, one wooden chair, a small side table with a bible and a small television. She notices the wash table with a water jug and bowl.

'No running water here, girls. Come on Gala you gotta help me do this.' He's set up at the table with a razor, scissors, towel and is taking off his shirt.

Gala unbraids his long hair slowly. She takes the scissors, tears filling her eyes as the shiny strands fall to the floor. She lathers up his scalp and shaves him carefully.

'I hope you don't lose your strength, honey, I love your hair.' She's sobbing quietly.

'Leah, turn on the TV.' Johnny, deep in thought, ignores his hairdresser.

The local news is on in Spanish. Johnny flashes on-screen with a picture of José. Tracy is being interviewed, *I knew he was trouble from the start. Them dirty Mexicans, trouble all day long.* Johnny's face darkens. He's very quiet. Gala tries to comfort him, putting her arms around his neck, kissing his shaved head, now shiny and cold.

'Okay, they've already been to the trailer park, babe. We gotta move fast, can't stay the night here. I'll go see about our IDs. You two stay right here, better you're not seen around town. You gals stand out like white lilies in a dark field.' He smiles at them. 'Don't let anyone in here, okay?' He leaves with his shades on.

Gala sweeps up Johnny's locks then stretches out on the bed while Leah giggles, watching the Flintstones in Spanish.

Johnny returns with a small quiet man, carrying a polaroid camera.

'He needs to take your pictures for the passports.'

'*Si, Señor, por favor.*' The photographer directs them and takes the shots, leaving as quietly as he arrived. Johnny flops down on the bed, his long legs dangling over the edge. 'Damn, these beds must be for short Mexicans.' He breathes a sigh. 'He'll be back soon, mija. And then we'll have to fly. I paid him top dollar to get them done pronto. Oh, by the way, my name is Steve now, Steve Adamson, a nice gringo name, on vacation with Janey Adamson, my wife. How do you like being Mrs Adamson, baby? Hey maybe we should get married in Mexico, what do ya think?'

'It's all going so fast, Johnny, like we're in a movie or something? You look totally different. We're on the run because you accidently killed someone. I have a new identity, we're fugitives now?' Gala hears the panic in her own voice.

There's a quiet tapping at the door and the photographer comes in with a manila envelope.

Gala checks out her passport. 'Mrs Janey Adamson, occupation, housewife. Gee, couldn't you have made me a bit more glamorous? A housewife? And Leah is Sadie now?'

'We gotta get into Mexico, we'll be safe over there. US cops can't touch me. The boys though, that's a whole nother story. Gotta do some praying to get through this.' Johnny reaches down and picks up Leah. 'Right, Miss Sadie?'

She reaches out and pats his smooth shiny bald head. 'No

hair for Johnny now, all gone.'

'Call me Steve, mija, I like that name now.'

The Cadillac slows down at the Mexican border. It's over a hundred degrees and the air is dusty. Johnny hands over their US passports.

'Purpose of your trip, Señor? Business or pleasure?'

'Pleasure, I'm on summer vacation with my family,' Johnny beams his winning smile.

'How much money do you have on you, Mr Adamson?'

'Four thousand US.'

'Where will you be staying in Mexico, Mr Adamson?'

'We'll be staying in Tampico for a two-week holiday.'

'Nice wheels, Señor. Y'all have a good time.'

The border policeman stamps their passports and they pass through the gates. Mr and Mrs Adamson are relieved and pretend everything is normal, for a moment. Johnny-Steve is all charged up and guns the Caddy into full speed, burning down the freeway south to Tampico. The radio is cranked up with a Santana track, which Johnny is singing to his new wifey.

'I got a black magic, woman.' He grins at her with a sparkle in his eye.

They pull into an old hotel on the beach, north of Tampico. Waves crash on the beach. Welcoming palm trees shush in the warm night air.

'I'm so ready to eat, Johnny-Steve,' Gala untangles her legs and opens the door.

'I'll go get us some local food and bring it to the room. Don't want to attract attention around here. You guys are so fair and foreign, it's so noticeable, babe.' Johnny opens the old wooden door to their room, which has a thatched roof. There's a simple table and chairs, a large bed and a hammock swinging in the corner.

'Don't be long, Johnny.'

'Can I sleep there, Mummy?' Leah has already climbed inside the multi-coloured woven hammock.

Gala rocks her girl back and forth slowly, listening to the waves crash on the white sand outside. The door opens and Johnny enters, his arms loaded with bags of piping hot food, which he lays out on the table.

'Enchiladas, rice, beans, corn tortillas, and chips, fresh salsa and guacamole. This is authentic Mexican *comida, mijas*. Wait until you taste this!'

'Almost as good as your mum's.' Gala dips into the guacamole.

'Got some primo smoke too, grown here, local killer bud, baby girl.'

Later Johhny and Gala are lying naked together, lights off and just the sound of the ocean lapping at the shore. Leah snores quietly in the hammock.

'I love every minute that we're together, Gala. You're true and so sweet to stay with me after all that's happened.' Johnny has his arms around her and is whispering in her ear.

'I just wish I could stay like this forever inside your strong arms, feeling your love,' Gala whispers.

'We have to live every second like there's no tomorrow, my beautiful Gala.'

'I'm trying, Johnny, really trying. It's exciting in a way but scary too. I don't know how it's all going to end and I don't ever want to lose you now.' She snuggles into him.

'I love you Gala and I want you to be my wife, really. I want you to have my son, a little brother for Leah?'

'That's what I want too. So wish it could come true. I'm writing a lovely poem about you, in my head. Have to write it down before I forget.'

'I'll grab you a writing book at our next stop. Keep those words coming, honey. It might be your best song yet. I can help you put it to music, okay? We've got to live in the now, mija. There's only this second, right now and our love right here, in this crummy border town, in this little shack of a hotel room. You and me loving each other. It's all there is, right now.'

They make love. The candlelight dances on the adobe walls. Leah is sleeping in the hammock. Later Johnny falls asleep, relaxed and beautiful. Gala sits up in bed, sounding the beginning of the poem quietly to herself.

I let you in
you the earth
I let you in
and now I cannot be inside
like Diana the hunter
I run under the purple sky
under the sacred moon
to the field that dreams
and lie and breathe with the world
And sing and laugh with the heavens
and know that God is smiling somewhere
and when the birds bring in the morning
I feel my bones and know I'm alive
Really alive

It's 4am in the small motel room in Tampico. Johnny is washing his face in the bowl and drying it with a thin white towel. Gala wakes up sleepy.

'We gotta get outta here, my *preciosa*. Come on get dressed, *andelez*. Get that sleepy little girl up too!' Johnny smiles at Leah curled up like a cat in the hammock.

Inside the Cadillac the sun is coming up, orange brush strokes across the sky. The ocean comes into view.

'Look, the beach. Mummy, can we go for a swim, pleeeease?'

'That's the Gulf of Mexico there, my honeys. We'll go for a swim soon, Leah, just past this town, okay?'

Johnny swings the Caddy behind the sheds down by a white beach and they all go for a swim. The water is turquoise, crystal and warm. Johnny grabs Gala playfully in the waves. He laughs and they kiss under the warm Mexican sun while Leah chases the waves, giggling, as they splash up around her.

'I'm counting my blessings right now.' Gala snuggles into Johnny's wet, brown skin.

He's looking up at the beach, watching some local teenagers pointing at his Texas license plates. Johnny's mood changes and they head back to the car. Inside the Cadillac, Gala dries Leah off with a white motel towel.

'I'll go get some food at the market and we'll stay out of

public view,' Johnny's tone is anxious.

'We could sleep in the car,' Gala says quietly.

'Yeah, we'll have to hide somewhere off the main road for a few days.'

Gala nods in agreement.

'You girls lie low and I'll go get some supplies.' Johnny pulls on a ball cap and shades, and strides off to the local *mercado*.

'Why do we have to stay in the car, Mummy? I want to go with Johnny-Steve. I want a lollipop, Mummy, please. When are we going to see my daddy? I want to see my real daddy.' Leah starts to cry.

'Quiet, Leah, Johnny will be back soon. We'll see your real daddy soon, okay. We're on a holiday now with Johnny.'

He comes back to the car with his arms full of groceries. 'I got cans of beans and corn so we can survive without a refrigerator for a few days. Okay, girls, get ready for a camping experience with camper Johnny, I mean camper Steve.' He laughs.

The Cadillac rumbles down a dirt road towards a white beach, deserted except for some tired looking horses chewing on dry grass. Johnny parks behind a falling down aluminium shed. Gala and Leah help him gather palm fronds to cover the car.

'It'll keep it cool too. Hey, girls, I bought you caps like mine!'

Johnny fits their 'I love Laredo' caps on, then opens a can of beans and salsa and hands the girls tortillas to scoop them up with. They sit down on the beach and savour the food, with the warm sand sifting in between their toes.

'I got some beers, and soda for the kid.'

'Thanks, darling, hey we could explore the beach and get some driftwood for a fire tonight, what do you think?'

'Yeah, good idea. We'll need a fire to keep away the hungry

coyotes and snakes.'

Gala and Leah look at each other at the mention of snakes. The three of them work together dragging branches into a pile for the night's bonfire.

'I'm tired now Mummy.'

'You've had such a big day, honey, swimming and helping gather wood. Look how your skin is turning brown,' Gala talks to Leah as she makes up a bed in the back of the Caddy and tucks her in.

'I wanted to see the fire, please, Mummy?' Leah says sleepily.

'Okay, sweetie, I love you.' Gala walks back to the beach where Johnny is making a huge fire with dry palm fronds. The sun is going down, stretching long golden fingers out across the bay.

'I feel safe in this little cove, Johnny. We're like castaways, deserted on a Caribbean Island. I just want to savour every minute I'm with you.' Gala watches him work, building up a sweat.

'I'm trying not to think about all that, just survival now, mija, survival.' He pokes at the palm fronds, making the flames crackle and the sparks leap out. 'How's this, baby: we can kick it here tonight, play guitars, make love by the fire? Whaddya say my little wifey? My little Janey Adamson?' Johnny lifts Gala up to kiss her and chuckles

'Sounds good to me, Johnny-Steve.'

'Watch out, baby. Get out of the way!'

Johnny pushes Gala aside, pulls his knife out and hurls it at a large rattlesnake backed up behind her. The silver knife gets the snake in the throat. Johnny crashes its head with a thick piece of driftwood. The snake lies lifeless in the sand. Gala is shaking and stares as Johnny cuts the snake's head off and lowers it into the flames, skewered on a sharp stick.

'More food for my family, snake is delicious! Burn baby, burn. Trying to hurt my *esposa* huh? I don't think so, Señor Snake. You okay, baby?'

'I've only ever seen a snake in the movies. That was bloody frightening.' Gala hugs Johnny. She's shaking.

'Don't worry I'm used to these suckers down here. Good to eat though. You wanna go get me some tortillas and beans, babe?'

Gala leaves Johnny to his camper Joe activities. He's fixing a grill with a chrome hubcap from the Caddy over the fire. Gala gets the food from the car and checks on Leah and looks for any evidence of snakes. She grabs a blanket and wraps it around her shoulders. She laughs when she sees the hubcap grill.

'Resourceful camper Johnny, Johnny on the run.'

'I don't think Tad would mind, do you? He pushes the snake meat round the grill.'

'No, I think he would probably do the same thing.' she refuses the snake meat he offers her. 'I'm happy with the tortillas and beans, though they do have a bit of a gas smell.'

'Watch the fire. I'll go get the beers and guitars.' Johnny strides back to the car.

Later in the evening Johnny's showing Gala a blues progression in E. 'Give it a Bo Diddley beat, babe, bump da bump da bump, da bump bump.'

Johnny beats out the rhythm on his guitar and Gala starts to play it.

'That's it, just keep going over and over. Hey I'll start recording our originals so we don't forget them, right?'

'This is fun. I'll get it down and I can put some words to it too,' says Gala.

Johnny solos over the progression and it sounds good in parts, although Gala is still trying to keep in time.

'Shoot, we could get some work together if we practised. You'll have to dye your hair, girl. It's too noticeable. You two stand out like *gringa turistas*. You could get a cowboy hat and blue jeans. You'll fit in now you two are getting tanned down here.'

'I've always wanted some real cowboy boots, blue and white ones.'

'Cowboy boots? Oh yeah, Janey the singing cowgirl, Yeeha!' Johnny puts his arms around Gala's waist, surrounding her with his body and love.

Three weeks later, Gala and Johnny are at a bar called South of the Border. They've been traveling down the coast, riding all day, busking and practising at night. Johnny has been recording the originals and now they have a good collection of songs: Gala's originals, Johnny's blues and some Spanish songs. Leah and Gala are now both tanned. Gala is developing the whole cowgirl look with a leather belt and turquoise buckle. Her hair has grown longer. Johnny's head is still shaved. He's talking to the owner, Ignacio, a broad Mexican man in his fifties with a kind, open face and bright welcoming smile. Gala is holding Leah's hand.

'We mostly play blues, Señor, in English and some in Spanish.'

'Okay, we'll try you guys out tonight for a couple of numbers, see how you go. You never know who's gonna show up in my bar. Sometimes my cousin Gabriel, from Mexico City comes to check out new talent. Yeah, he's a bigshot DJ from the main radio station back there. So, around nine, Señor?'

Johnny is pleased and they go back to the car, 'Come on, cowgirl. We gotta get our shit together.'

A few hours later Gala puts on her new jeans, cowboy shirt and fixes her new powder blue cowboy hat over her dyed shiny black hair. Leah is asleep in the back seat. 'What are we going to do with Leah, Johnny? We can't take her to the bar.'

'She'll be alright, baby. I'll find someone to watch the car, pay them a few dollars.' Johnny locks the car and they walk to the bar. Gala looks back at the sleek Cadillac, parked up next to the dusty curb with her precious baby inside. Her stomach tightens. 'It's only a couple of songs,' she tells herself. A motorbike tears past, spitting up dust. She tightens her grip on the guitar case and prays that Johnny's right, this time.

Inside and on stage, Johnny asks Gala how she likes the mic. He adjusts it and counts in the first song, Denton. The owner smokes a cigar at the bar and nods his head to the beat at times.

South of the Border has all the character of a Mexican Cantina, lit with lanterns and tall candles. The polished dark wood counter has real leather bar stools. The tables are tiled in turquoise and burnt sienna with leather barrel chairs. Wooden bowls of taco chips and salsa are placed, ready for customers.

Delicious aromas are coming from the kitchen - fried chicken, tortillas, beans, cumin and cilantro. It reminds Gala how hungry she is.

In the next song, 'Romance Junkie,' the owner chuckles at the lyrics and taps his foot to the catchy Bo Diddley beat.

If I don't see you for one day it feels like three,
Need a fix of your loving to satisfy me
'Cause I'm a romance junkie and I got the blues
Yes, I love you baby, I love you.

After the song ends, the bar owner approaches the stage.

'Yep, that's good stuff, you're a hell of a guitar player, Steve. Been playing long?'

Johnny's enjoying the reaction, 'Yeah a few years now.'

'Well, my name's Ignacio and I'm the owner of this little place.' Ignacio is a broad, handsome Mexicano with a wide welcoming smile and glossy dark eyes. 'You guys can have the Thursday night spot, the New Talent night. Can you do a full set this week?'

'Two sets, no sweat. I'm Steve Adamson and this is my wife, Janey.' Johnny is fully in charge and pleased at the outcome.

'Okay, fifty bucks for two sets, plus dinner and some beers. How's that, Señor Adamson?'

'Sounds good to me.' He shakes the owner's hand firmly.

'You've got a great voice, missy, real soulful. People like that around here, especially that country song.' Ignacio winks at her and walks back to the bar.

Johnny and Gala pack up their gear.

'I can't believe we got hired just like that, plus dinner and drinks.' She reaches up and kisses Johnny.

'No big deal really, I'm used to getting gigs. I told you, you could sing, babe. Listen we should get a room here in town, stay awhile. We're farther south now and I need a rest from all that driving.'

'Sounds great to me, settle down a little? That would be a lovely change. Leah would like it too.' She makes a beeline to the door to see her daughter.

Inside yet another adobe motel with a thatch roof by the ocean, Johnny checks all the walls and corners for scorpions and they settle in. There's a goat chewing grass out back. They tune up their guitars and dress for the gig. Johnny polishes up their boots and whistles happily.

Back at South of the Border, Johnny and Gala are setting up when she notices some well-dressed strangers sitting at a table by the stage. They are in expensive suits and ties – executive look. Ignacio comes over. 'Those city dudes down there have come in to check out new talent. Actually, one of them's my cousin Alejandro. He's been at some big shot promotion thing. Yeah, he and his buddy Gabriel are from that top radio station in Mexico City I was telling you about. I told them about you two. They're keen to hear your country original, so sock it to them, guys!' He's pleased with himself.

Gala starts with Denton and notices the feet of the well-dressed men tapping along. Johnny rips into a great solo.

At the end of their set, Ignacio comes up to the stage. 'My cousin, Alex, wants you to do your first song again. Denton, was it? One more time please, Janey. Said they'd buy y'all a drink and they want to meet you.' He chuckles. 'They've never heard anybody from Down Under sing before.'

Gala sings with her heart, giving it her best under the intent gaze of the DJs.

Daughter lay there sleeping
Phoenix moon hung low
Just me and my dreaming
So much I didn't know
Thinking how my man would feel
Coming home after work
Finds the note I have written tears streaming the dirt
I didn't mean to hurt him so
All I knew was I had to go

Gala and Johnny walk over to the table. The men stand.

'You write that last song, Miss?' one of them asks.

'I just finished it really.' Gala is shy.

'We think that song's a winner, girl. With the right production and your man here on the guitar you got a hit! Do you have management?' The man smiles at Gala.

'No, not really, we just started playing together really.'

Alejandro reaches out his hand, takes Gala's and kisses it with old fashioned charm.

'*Mucho gusto, Señorita*, my name is Alejandro. You can call me Alex.'

'Janey,' she takes her hand back, avoiding his deep gaze.

Johnny is talking enthusiastically to Gabriel in Spanish, then takes Gala aside. 'Guess what, honey, these guys think we should record your Denton song. Isn't that great?'

'Really? I can't believe it. It's too good to be true.' Gala is steadying herself, giddily happy.

'We want you guys to come up to Mexico City to record, okay? We can arrange the drummer and bass player and can handle distribution and all that stuff.' Gabriel is so sincere.

'We're one of the top stations in the city, KMAL. We like to showcase new talent, especially from overseas,' Alex adds with enthusiasm.

Johnny looks pleased but a little tense at the mention going to Mexico City.

'We really want to stay in this town for a bit longer. Couldn't we record somewhere closer?' Gala asks, realising Johnny could get stopped at the airport.

'Well, we could arrange somewhere else I suppose, Janey. I'll look into it.' The men exchange a look.

'Look,' Johnny jumps in, 'It's just me. I need to stay here for personal reasons. Janey can go. It's her song.' He turns to Gala, 'baby, you should go. It's a great chance and you gotta take them when they come along. Do it.'

Gala is shocked. It's mind-blowing, but without Johnny? She watches him, checking out his reaction.

He jumps up. 'Let's do another set, mija.'

Back on-stage Johnny rips into an amazing riff that fills up the room and takes them all on a smooth journey upwards. The guitar is howling and singing with more strength than ever. He's showing Gala how he feels and how much his heart aches for her, his pride. At the end of the set, they pack up quietly, knowing things are about to change.

The DJs come up to Gala after the set. 'Janey, could you fly with us to Mexico City tomorrow? We want to jump right on this thing. Strike while the iron's *caliente*,' Gabriel's intensity, driving the mission.

'I'd love to, but I have to make arrangements for my daughter. She's only four.'

'No problema,' says Alex, 'I have family in Mexico City. My sister can watch her. I'll ask her. Settled then?'

He shakes Gala's hand fiercely. His tanned forehead is beading with sweat, eyes too shiny.

Mexico City, August, 1975

Inside the Mexicana airplane, Gala shows Leah how to snap her seat belt into place. Leah is by the window. Alex and the moustached Gabriel, are in the aisle across from them, waving and giving the thumbs up.

'What corny guys. Look at them, like the cat with the cream or something,' Gala whispers to her daughter.

'Can we have some peanuts, Mummy?'

'Okay sweetie, wanna soft drink?'

The plane takes off and they are soon zooming over the candyfloss clouds and it all looks like Toytown below. Leah has her face pressed up to the window.

The air stewardess comes smiling down the aisle, '*Una cervesa y soda por favor, y?*' Gala asks, pointing to the peanuts not knowing what they are called in Spanish.

'*Botana de cacahuates?* Here, Señorita.' The stewardess hands Gala a few packets and winks at Leah.

La Vida es un regalo

The plane passes over a blue mountaintop.

'Mexico City in forty-five minutes!' Alex calls out to Gala.

Descending into Mexico City, Gala sees miles and miles of slums and tent towns. Families are squatting around small fires in the dry ground. The central city looms up. Castles, cathedrals and a perfect square in the main centre.

'There's our town square, Janey, not long now.' Alex sounds excited.

Outside the Mexico City airport, an impressive limousine waits for them - long, black and shiny with a uniformed driver who opens the door with style. Gala is beginning to feel like a celebrity.

Alex gets in beside Gala, 'We've put you in the Grand Hotel in the square, Janey. You'll love it! *Muy bonita!*' Alex pats her hand reassuringly.

Gabriel is on the car phone talking excitedly in Spanish, mentioning Janey's name.

'It's all set. You're in the studio, *mañana*, at noon. How's that for service?' Gabriel is beaming with super white teeth.

'Wow, very fast! I'll do my best for you guys. Thanks so much.'

'And tonight, we'll take you out to dinner to celebrate! How about it, honey?' Alex is excited, wiping dripping beads of sweat from his shiny brow with a silk handkerchief.

'Not too late though, we want your voice to be good for recording, mija,' Gabriel has a worried tone and seems to be the more sensible of the two.

Inside the Grand Hotel, a porter appears to take their bags. Gala's bag and guitar are quickly put on the trolley with Leah giggling on top. The Porter opens the hotel door, a majestic, gilt, ornately carved affair with a huge bronze doorknob. It glides open to reveal the foyer with gleaming marble floors and chandeliers. Huge bouquets of birds of paradise adorn the reception desk.

Alex speaks to the concierge, taking the keys and putting one in his pocket. 'We'll pick you up pronto at 8 pm. We can leave your *muchacha* with my sister Katrina, call her Kata. She's an excellent hairstylist and lives close to here. She has two little *niños*.' He kisses her on the cheek and presses the other room key into her palm. Alex is definitely in charge.

Inside Gala's hotel suite, the bellhop places her belongings on the ornate ottoman. She pays him some *centavos*, unsure what is the correct amount for a tip. Leah is running around checking out the room. It's quite ostentatious, with gold and bronze everywhere, even chandeliers. The double bed is made of puffy burgundy velvet and covered with fluffy pink cushions. There's a well-stocked minibar and a range of taco chips and snacks.

Leah's already jumping on the double bed and laughing. 'Look, Mummy, they've got TV!'

'I know, darling. To think we were frying tortillas on a hubcap just a few weeks ago? We've come a long way, baby. Now you go jump on that little bed. That's your one.'

'Okay, Mummy. Is Johnny-Steve going to stay with us?'

'Not this time darling,' Gala says sadly. She suddenly misses him and thinks of their last night together, a mixture of love and parting, holding each other tightly. Leah's jumping is making her irritable. 'Leah, can you settle down please? See what's on TV? Mummy has to get dressed and we're going out soon.'

'Am I going with you?'

'You're going to stay at Alex's sister's place. Kata, she has two kids around your age. Won't that be fun?'

Leah is not so sure but settles down to watch Mexican cartoons. Gala showers in the luxurious pink marble bathroom and wraps up in a pink robe, drying her dark hair with a big thick pink towel. She checks out the mini bar, which has over fifty small liquors and a range of beers, soda and wine. She pours a cola for Leah and pours herself a Bohemia beer, enjoying the cold rich lager, finally relaxing alone with her daughter in a luxurious setting. They really do seem to have come a long way.

Katrina opens the door to her house, round, friendly, motherly, her youngest child bouncing on her hip.

'Don't worry,' Alex says. 'She'll be fine. Kata's great with kids.'

The limo slides through the cobblestone streets and stops outside a marble courtyard. Gala and Alex are ushered through to an exclusive table, in an upmarket seafood restaurant.

'They have the best lobster in the whole city. We pick them out ourselves. Do you like lobster?' Alex is following the maître-d.

'Well, we have crayfish back home. I've had them before. Is Gabriel joining us?'

'Nah he's got some family thing on.' Alex appears to be blushing. 'He has a huge family, seven brothers and at least four sisters. Huge, *ay Dios*, eleven kids! Don't worry. I'll keep you amused.' He winks slyly.

'This way, Señor,' the maître-d leads them into a secluded booth. He lights the tall beeswax candles and closes the heavy velvet curtains. Immediately the wine waiter appears and takes their order. He quickly returns with a bottle of chilled sparkling white wine, a special reserve Spanish wine, Cava, which he serves with old world charm and style.

'Gosh, bubbles and lobster. It's unreal.' Gala is overwhelmed.

'Let's toast to our hit record, baby, number one. Come on, we have to go pick our lobster.' Alex looks happy.

They go to a huge tank filled with live lobsters. Gala watches the lobsters, imprisoned in the tank and feels bad for them.

'Get a nice big one,' Alex tells her, 'Here, look that one has plenty of flesh on it.'

'It seems a bit barbaric, choosing which trapped lobster shall die, in such an opulent setting, don't you think?'

He's not listening to her.

The seductive dinner continues with a tasty array of platters: carnitas, fresh salsa, gazpacho and soft white tortillas. Alex is getting very merry with the Cava.

'Señor, over here. More of that *delicioso* wine over here.' He orders another bottle of Cava to go with the lobster and keeps topping Gala's glass up. He chatters excitedly about the project. The wine is going to Gala's head. She feels dreamy and pleasant listening to Alex rabbit on. 'I'm going with the whole country girl cowgirl look. That's so sexy! Your song's in a country style too. It all works. It's a number one hit, *numero uno*.'

'This lobster just melts in your mouth. I've never tasted such a succulent flesh.'

'Just like you, babe, succulent and sweet to taste, I bet.'

Gala ignores this remark and her attention fades in and out of his rave. She feels bad that Johnny is missing out on all this feast. Dessert follows with yet another waiter and a divine fruit and cream parfait.

'This is one of the most exquisite dinners. I've ever had in my life, Alex,' Gala slurs. 'Honestly incredible. I wish Johnny, I mean Steve, could have come with us. I think I better get back to the hotel now.' She feels woozy.

'Sure, baby, right after our espresso, you want an espresso, don't you?'

'Why not?' Gala sighs.

Outside the hotel the limousine stops.

'Wait here, hombre. I'll see the señorita to her room.'

Inside the Grand Hotel, Alex guides Gala past the concierge desk and up the stairs, opening the door with his own key.

Gala goes to show him out. 'Thanks for such a lovely dinner and everything Alex.'

'Not so fast, Janey. What's the rush? I want to do a line, do you like coke?'

'Actually, I've never tried it. Jo… Steve does sometimes, but it gets him all hyped up.'

'This is some smooth Colombian shit, baby, pure.' Alex is convincing. 'One line and it'll wake you up. You'll be ready to party!'

'What the hell.' Gala takes off her tall platforms as Alex cuts two lines of coke on the glass table with a silver pocketknife. He rolls up a red Mexican bill and offers it to Gala.

'Well, my mother always told me it's polite to take the one that's closest.' She giggles, tiddly, then snorts the line. It hits Gala was such a rush. The shapes in the room all come into sharp focus. Alex follows suit. His line is a gagger.

'This will mellow you out, girl, see?'

'I feel really numb actually. Can't feel my lips. I think I'm mellow, but I'm just too numb to tell.'

Alex slips off his Italian loafers and checks out the mini bar, making himself at home. 'Co'rrele, my favourite. Gran Marnier! You wanna join me for a liqueur?'

'Why stop now?' Her voice seems to be far away and she plonks herself down on the overstuffed over pillowed couch.

Alex, the mover, joins her in seconds, with Brandy snifters of the sweet orange liqueur. As they sip, he moves closer towards her, his manicured hands are on her bare leg whenever he emphasises his point.

'Get used to this, cowgirl. Champagne-living every night. *Numero Uno!*'

Laughing Alex swings round and kisses Gala fully on the mouth. She tries to push him off, but he's tall and strong and his knee wedges her legs open. He rips down her underwear.

'No, no, Alex, not this. Stop. Please!'

She feels his hot breath on her neck and she can't push him off.

'Please stop. Alex. You know I have a boyfriend... husband. This isn't right. Please stop!' Gala is scared at what's happening and powerless to stop him. His strong arms pin her down.

'I'm too turned on now, baby girl. You got such a cute little ass, I just want to get into you. I'll be careful, I promise. Please I can't stop now.'

Alex forces himself into Gala and starts fucking her really hard and aggressively, his face above her, like a dark hungry wolf. Gala keeps struggling, but that seems to excite him more, and he goes at it harder and harder. She starts to cry.

'Don't you cry, bitch! You like it? Tell your daddy you like it. You do, oh baby.' He gets up and slaps Gala on her bare behind. 'How is that? Pretty sexy night, huh? Get used to it, *Numero Uno.*'

Gala gets up, too numb to reply. She goes into the bathroom. Her mascara is running down her face and she sees in the mirror, a love bite like a bruised rose on her neck.

'Fucking bastard.' She stays in the bathroom, numbly

washing herself. When she comes back to the room, Alex has let himself out. There's Mexican bills and a line of coke on the glass bedside table. Gala falls onto the bed sobbing, wishing Johnny was with her.

The next morning on the balcony of the Grand Hotel, Gala takes her morning espresso. She watches the flag folding ceremony, an event performed daily by uniformed soldiers in perfect precision. She sips the coffee and looks down at the square, sore and dazed from the night, feeling alone and foolish to have been so naïve. She takes out her notebook and finishes her poem about Johnny.

Let my tears run tiny ribbons on your riverbank eyes.
Open them to the skies, come die with me.
Come with me to the praying tree.
In the wild, honey fields end it with me.
Kneel with me on the crumbling Earth.
Pray with me.
End it with me.
And pray as I kiss your face.
Cold with tears.
'Neath the praying tree.
Pray as I kiss your face.
Kiss you forever, 'neath the praying tree.

and now I'm like
Diana the Hunter
I cannot be inside
and run under the
purple sky
To the field that dreams
And lie and breathe
with the world and
know that God is
smiling somewhere

and pray
as I kiss your face
cold with tears
'neath the praying tree
Pray as I kiss your
face

kiss your
forever
'neath the
Praying Trees

Come with me
to the praying tree
in the wild honey
and it with me

kneel with me
on the crumbling earth
Pray with me
and it with me

Seljak '24

Recording Session at KMAL 1975

Inside the limo, Gala covers the dark rose love bite on her neck with the turquoise handkerchief that Johnny gave her for good luck. She's sitting in between Alex and Gabriel, who are raving in Spanish.

Gala quietly interrupts them. 'I want to talk to Leah, please.'

'Sure, no problema.' Alex dials the carphone and gets Kata, then Leah on the phone.

'Hi, Mummy, when are you coming over here?'

'Soon, darling, after I finish my recording, I'll come and get you then, okay? Be good and I'll bring you a treat. Okay, darling?'

'Yeay for mummy. I miss you. Love you, bye.'

The studio at KMAL is large and spacious with top-of-the-line recording equipment. A young, focussed Mexican drummer is setting up in a soundproof booth and a handsome black bass player is practising runs on a fretless Gretsch. Gala greets them shyly, wishing Johnny were there to help her communicate with them.

'Hola, guys.'

The bass player nods approvingly and smiles. He seems friendly and very competent.

Alex is buzzing all around the studio like an annoying mosquito. Gala wishes he would just leave them to get on with it. She ignores him and tunes up.

'Okay, give it your best shot. Sing your sexy song just for me, Janey girl.' He looks high already.

The bass player eyes the drummer, and they're ready to go.

Gabriel is inside the sound booth. 'Just run through the song, Janey. Plug your guitar into that DI box and go through it one time, Okay?'

Gala sings her song, closing her eyes and picturing Johnny. Sadness comes up and tears fill her eyes.

'Wow, that's a sad song, girl.' The bass player shakes his head as he figures out some cool runs.

'Okay, we're ready to try a live run. The vocal will just be a practise. Tapes rolling.' Gabriel is on top of it.

Gala gains strength from the solid groove that the bass player and drummer have laid down and sings her song again.

'That's a take. That's a good take. Will work on the rhythm section, and then you can do another vocal. Can you do b/vs, Janey? *Bueno muchacha, bueno!*' Gabriel is elated. Gala's pleased with the reaction.

'Yeah, I could work out something I suppose.' She smiles at the musicians. 'Hey thanks, you guys sound great.'

The studio door bursts open and Alex is there with arms outstretched, beaming madly. '*Córrele*, star!'

Gala grabs her guitar and follows him numbly down the dark hall to listen to the playback. Inside there are coloured lights, studio lights blinking. The rhythm tracks kick in as the door closes.

'You did great! *Numero uno*, baby, all the way!'

Gala is quiet.

'What's the matter, star? Are you upset with Alejandro about last night? Don't be mad at me, Princess. You're as much to blame, wearing that sexy mini, and I had all that coke. I just couldn't help myself.'

Gala cannot believe he's defending himself, like he was entitled. 'I have a bad headache actually and I need a little quiet now.'

'No problema. Wanna do a line?'

'I want my voice to be natural. Just some aspirin, okay?'

'Yeah, you're right. I'll get some Tylenol. I'll be right back.'

He sprints off in his too-tight jeans and loafers. Gala crashes on the leather couch in the lounge area. Mexican pop magazines, a backgammon set and a smeared mirror clutter the coffee table. Alex reappears suddenly with a packet of extra strength Tylenol and grabs a coke from the fridge.

'Here, baby, you're gonna feel better real soon, my star. I'll do a line though, keep on to it, huh, keep the star energy up?'

He lines up another gagger and snorts it up loudly. Gala is finding his fidgety behaviour annoying and wishes he would just go away and leave her alone. He sits down really close to her on the couch and she moves away.

He stands up. 'Listen, you gringa bitch. I'm paying for this whole recording. You owe me and you better start being a bit more friendly, or you'll regret it.' He grabs Gala's shirtfront, pulling her up from the couch. 'Everyone's dispensable in this business, baby!' he spits out at her. 'Even you, *preciosa, comprendes*?'

Alex slams the door hard as he leaves the lounge. Gala falls back on the couch, feeling like a cheap whore, not a quality recording artist. She sobs like a child, shaking and afraid.

◦─◦◦○◦◦─◦

Sometime later she is woken by Gabriel. 'Come on, Janey, we're ready for you now. The boys have done a great job. Wait'll you hear your song, cowgirl.'

The sound booth is bubbling as Janey sits in the swivel chair. The bass and drums are good together and she's pleased her guitar part sounds solid and chunky.

'All that's missing is some lead in that break, and we've got something.' Gabriel seems very happy with the sound.

'Okay, baby, go give it your all-time best now.' Alex opens the door to the vocal booth.

Gala doesn't look at him. She puts on the headphones and adjusts them so she can still hear her own voice and pitch.

'Okay, I'm ready now, Gabriel.'

'*Uno, dos, tres*, tape's rolling.'

Gala closes her eyes and really gives it her best shot, thinking of Johnny, imagining him playing in the solo break.

'That's a really good take. Wanna listen to it?' Gabriel is beaming.

'Yeah, okay.' Gala goes into the sound booth and everyone's smiling, even the musicians.

'I think we might have this song in the can, one time Charlie.' Alex tries to put his arm around Gala. She moves away and stands by the bass player. At the end of the track, she's pleased.

'I'm happy with it, guys. I could do another take? The vocal sounds warm. It sounds like me, only richer.'

'We'll sort out the guitar lead later. We've got the goods in the can now.' Gabriel beams up at her.

Gala nods, suddenly tired. She wants her daughter and desperately wants to go home to Johnny right away.

At the airport in Mexico City, Alex slips a cassette tape into Gala's hand as she gets ready to board the plane, Leah and guitar in tow.

'Check this out, *numero uno*. We'll be in touch,' he says.

The engine wakes Gala and Leah as the plane touches down.

Gala scans the waiting faces, looking for Johnny and then he strides over smiling. He picks up Leah and kisses Gala all at once.

'How did it all go, mija?'

'The recording went pretty smooth. I have a tape to listen to. Baby, I'm so happy to see you.'

Johnny holds Gala close in the midst of all the other passengers pushing past. His warm love is a shield against the world, the bustling crowd squeezing past them, blurry- shapes. Time stops still. Gala feels the warmth from his body caressing her. Nothing else matters.

'Come on Gala. We better get back. You look tired. You sure you're okay?'

'Yeah, it was a lot of pressure. You know, new for me recording and everything and I really missed you.'

Inside the Cadillac, Johnny slips the cassette inside the car stereo. They drive as Gala's song plays. Gala looks ahead, watching the road, turning shyly and catching Johnny smiling and listening. He looks at her proudly when it ends.

'That's a great track baby. Your voice sounds beautiful. You could have a winner there. Hey, that lead guitar sounds pretty hot. Where did you find him?'

'I don't know. They added that track after I left the studio.'

'I helped you out there.' He chuckles. 'I slipped that DJ a tape I recorded on the road and he's used a solo from that. He's cleaned it up. Sounds pretty cool actually. *Ay Dios mio*, the wonders of modern technology.' Johnny is pretty pleased with himself.

'I had no idea. That's great you're on it after all.'

She relaxes into the solace of Johnny's shoulder and settles into the ride back to the motel.

Early in the morning inside the motel, Gala hears the scraping of boots at the door and she wakes Johnny.

'Listen, someone is out there,' she whispers.

He gets up and is pulling on his jeans when the motel door bursts open. Jesús and David stagger in. Jesús is drunk and has a Colt 45 pulled on Johnny. Gala screams.

'This is for José, *chingara madre. Vengara* for José!'

The first shot blasts out, hitting Johnny in the chest. He falls down, and then tries to get up, dark red blood spreading across his chest.

Gala is screaming and crying.

'Don't do this. Jesús, don't do this, *hermano*!' Johnny is pleading.

Jesús shoots him again. This bullet hits Johnny in the forehead and he goes down hard.

Jesús is crying, in shock at what he's just done.

Gala runs to help Johnny. 'No more, Jesús, you've killed him. You've killed my Johnny. Please stop. Stop!' She shields her love, cradling him. The world stops all around her. There's no sound as she rocks him. 'My sweet, sweet baby. I love you, Johnny Magana.' She doesn't even hear Leah sobbing.

Everything goes dark around Gala. There is nothing, no meaning, no life, only darkness.

Viaje solitario, September 1975

Inside the Cadillac, Gala's driving north on the freeway. Leah's up-front chatting happily away. *I'm on autopilot*, thinks Gala,

Gala keeps her eyes on the road ahead and uses her sleeve to wipe her face, which is damp with tears.

'Are we going to see my daddy now, Mummy?'

Gala doesn't know how to answer. She doesn't know what's ahead for her and her brave, resilient daughter. But she does know that she can't go back to her old life with Billy. She flicks on the radio and finds a station. The Texan DJ drawls, 'This is a new track from a fresh new talent! A young songwriter all the way from Down Under, New Zealand. Have a listen. We think this track's a winner!'

I never meant to hurt him, so
All I knew was I had to go.
And there's nothing so lonesome
Nothing quite so sad
Than pulling into Denton at midnight
With your whole life in a bag.'

Gala smiles, hearing Leah is quietly singing along with the song. She reaches out and smoothes her daughter's hair.

'If I keep writing songs and taking good care of you my darling girl, I think we're going to be okay. We'll see your daddy soon, honey.'

The sun is setting and splashes colour over the Mojave Desert. The beams stretch out like the long, golden fingers of God towards the endless flat horizon.

glossary

Abuela: grandmother
Adobe: bricks made from clay
Amigo: friend
Andele: hurry up
Angelitos: little angels
Authentico: authentic
Ay Dios mio: my God
Bebe: baby
Bohemian: a popular Mexican beer
Botana de cacahuates: peanuts
Buena: good
Cabrón: literally goat, but slang for motherfucker, also used as and endearment between men
Centavos: Mexican cents
Cervesa: beer
Casa: house or home
Chingada madre: motherfucker
Cocina: kitchen
Comida: food
Co'rrele: come on
Crackers: pejoritive term for southern white folks, similar to redneck
Deliciosa: delicious
Dinero: money
Ese: slang term for man
Familia: family
Frijoles: refried beans
Gato: cat
Gracias: thank you

Gringa: white girl (slang/ derogatory)

Gringo: white guy (slang/ derogatory

Hermana: sister

Hermano: brother

Hola: hello

Hombre: man

Inglés: English

Loco: crazy

Mamacita: literally little mother but slang for hot mama

Mañana: morning

Mariachi: traditional Mexican folk music

Mercado: market/shop

Mija: literally daughter, but also a term of endearment like sweetheart

Molinillo: traditional turned wooden whisk for making hot chocolate

Mota: slang term for cannabis

Muchacha: girl

Muchacho: boy

Mucho gusto: pleasure, as in 'it's a pleasure to meet you'

Muy: very

Niños: boys

No hablo inglés: I don't speak English

Numero uno: number one

Otro lado: literally on the other side, a slang reference to the Mexican border

Pan dulce: sweet Mexican pastries

Pobrecito: poor little thing

Pinche: literally kitchen hand, but slang for cheap or fucking

Poco limón: a little bit of lemon

Por favor: please

Pollitos: chickens

Preciosa: precious, beautiful, lovely

Que pasa?: what's happening?

Que tu quieres?: what do you want?

Sangre: blood

Señor: Sir or Mister

Señorita: Miss

Serape: colourful Mexican blanket

Socorro: help

Tecate: a popular Mexican beer displaying the United Farmworkers' black eagle emblem

Trabajo: work

Uno, dos, tres: one, two, three

Vamonos: let's go

Vengara: to avenge/ revenge

Y'all: plural form of you, used in southern states in the US, but also used in west Texas as a polite singular: 'y'all okay, Miss.'

list of paintings by Katy Soljak
Acrylic on Canvas 2015-2022

Cover and Page 72/73: *Blood Moon over Quadalupe,* 51 cm x 102 cm

Page 13: *Greyhound Crossing the Mojave,* 61 cm x 91 cm

Page 18: *Gala Calling Denton,* 76 cm x 51.5 cm

Page 20: *Trace,* 51 cm x 45 cm

Page 24: *Tad,* 92 cm x 46, 5 cm

Page 26: *Love 1970 - Crypt Nightclub Auckland,* 75.5 cm x 101.5 cm

Page 31: *Tad's Caddy,* 36 cm x 45.5 cm

Page 35: *Leah and Cindy Try Texas Ice Cream,* 25.5 cm x 25.5 cm

Page: 45 *Johnny Magana,* 45.5 cm x 61 cm

Page 68/69: *Poolroom Fracas,* 61 cm x 122 cm

Page 80/81: *Gabriela's Cocina,* 45.5 cm x 91.5 cm

Page 87: *Desert Dreaming,* 76 cm x 102 cm

Page 89: *Quadalupe Marron,* 31 cm x 15.5 cm

Page 110: *Gala and Johnny at South of the Border Bar,* 101.5 cm x 101.5 cm

Page 113: *La Vida es un Regala,* 76 cm x 61 cm

Page 121: *Praying Tree,* 101.5 cm x 101.5 cm

Page 129: *Viaje Solitario,* 101.5 cm x 101.5 cm

Katy Soljak is a writer, musician, singer-song writer and artist, living on Waiheke Island. In the late eighties she moved to California where she studied creative writing at Long Beach Community College. She then became involved with the LB poetry scene, reading poetry on trains and in laundromats with the Carma Bums. She performed regularly in the nineties in Los Angeles and Long Beach, was a featured poet at Beyond Baroque in Venice Beach and was published in On Target, Pearl and Brainchild. Katy began writing short stories when she retired from teaching in 2008. They have variously been read on the radio or published in literary journals. She still performs songs and poetry at 'The Song and Poetry Thing' on Waiheke Island. Her debut short story collection, *My First Real Pash and Other Stories*, was published by Lasavia Publishing in 2021. Her songs featured in this novella, *Denton* and *Heaven,* are available for download from Spotify and iTunes.